Heartlight

Annie Renfay

authorHOUSE®

AuthorHouse™
1663 Liberty Drive, Suite 200
Bloomington, IN 47403
www.authorhouse.com
Phone: 1-800-839-8640

First published by AuthorHouse 1/19/2009

ISBN: 978-1-4389-3685-7 (sc)

*Printed in the United States of America
Bloomington, Indiana*

This book is printed on acid-free paper.

Table of Contents

Acknowledgements

To my assistant, Zackary Oliver:
From each idea and bit of your genius-filled writing that
went into this book to your encouragement which helped me
to keep going, I immensely enjoyed having you work with
me on this project. Whenever I was stuck or felt like it just
wasn't worth continuing, I'd pick up the phone, and there
you were, helping me through my block and telling me that
Heartlight is really all that I want it to be.

To the editor, Sandy Blair:
A big thank-you for all the time and effort you have put into
making sure this production is glitch-free. You have played
a big part in making this book what it is today. It was a
pleasure working with you, and I greatly appreciate it.

To my Dad, Mom, and Gracie:
I am so blessed to have such a great family. Thank you for
all your support and for being understanding.

To friends Rachel Peiffer, Kristy Williams, Susan Wiersema,
Daniel McCaskill, Karen Fu, and Kelsey Cooksey:
A writer's first fans will always hold a special place in
heart. Thank you.

1
Cups and Saucers

The trumpets sounded as they always did when someone of importance entered or exited the palace grounds by the main gates. Duquesa Meria burst into the entrance of the duque's palace in Royaleh with the loyal royal luggage bearers trailing behind.

"Where's Arlend?!?!" the typically poised and rational lady hollered, her voice echoing through the grand hall. She had just arrived after spending several weeks in the Green Hills of Fenalla far to the south, the news of the events which took place amidst the swamp and the bay being the first to reach her ears upon return.

The face of Duque Jovell, whose command of the country was second only to the king, appeared in the doorway of the hall. "Honey..." he started nervously, his brow furrowing, the one sign of age among his features which boated of his youthful appearance which was common among Highlanders. Though well over a thousand years of age, he looked to be in his early thirties. "Let me explain…"

"Answer. My. Question. First." Meria glowered. There were only two people in all Myrada who could speak to the duque in this manner, one was the king. The other was currently exercising her abilities to the max. Their offspring, the marques and marquesas, who had come to greet the duquesa, were starting to eye each other nervously, for their brother Arlend had been in bed since his ordeal.

"He...he's in his bed," Duque replied.

"He's *dead*!" she wailed.

"No, darling, he's just - "

"You killed him!"

"Meria! I would do no such - "

"Oh, Jovell, tell me it isn't true. The shockwave? At my Arlend?"

"Now, honey - "

She collapsed onto a couch and started sobbing, her normally energetic, auburn curls falling limp to cover her face. Arlend's siblings, who ranged from Marco, at six years younger than Arlend's some 190 years of age or so, to little Rosie, who was but six, were all clustered at the bottom of the stairs.

(This was before elevators.) They now stood still, expressions of worry written on all their faces, silently noting that it had been nearly a month since they last saw their brother. Like all the Highlanders of the world of Myrada, they could live for many millenniums on end and never look to be older than 20 or 30 or so, and had the ability to run faster, see and hear farther, and heal themselves. This was a contrast to the Mainlanders, the mortals who lived across the ocean with life spans and abilities like you and I here on Earth. But all this ability, plus their other talents were not needed for any of them to know that they best retreat back up the stairs; which they did soundlessly.

~*~*~*~*~*~*~*~

Time meant little during the serene, content moments just between the peaceful stillness of sleep and the refreshed awareness of awakening. The afternoon sun slipped in through the edges of drawn curtains veiling the large windows, casting a subtle, caressing glow upon the furniture in the spacious bedroom on the fifth floor of the east wing of the duque's palace. On the west side of the room, Marque Arlend smiled in his sleep. The time was just right – he was wakeful enough to enjoy it, yet unconscious enough to dream. Conscious as necessary to relish in the intensity of how he so often longed for these moments, yet sufficiently asleep to not take into mind the fact it would end all too soon.

Arlend breathed deeply. He could feel her presence alive within him, an illusion of all that he desired. And had desired for so long. He had met her for a few, precious hours; though he was grateful he even got that many. Yet those fleeting moments were enough for her to become like his own child to him. Enough for him to form an attachment with her that he felt he would never be able to break.

Closer than a sister, more dear than any friend. Arlend knew at that moment he should never have a daughter…Try as he might, she would inevitably be compared to *this*… Everything about her was too perfect, almost surreal…He replayed the melody of her laughter once more in his head. Her cute, melodious giggle was like a babbling brook, music to his ears.

From the beginning, his instincts had told him that it was too good to be true, too marvelous to last. Arlend felt he was glowing with joy as he saw her smile beneath his eyelids. Her pale skin, like a moonlit path, framed by her long, sandy hair complemented her sparkling, blue eyes which were lit by her small, angelic smile... The smile that he would never again be able to see.

'I need to stop shaking. Stop *shaking*, or I'll drop these groceries and get beaten!'

Arlend's eyes blinked open.

'Steady now, steady.'

Arlend couldn't believe it, he was going insane. The little girl was speaking in his head.

"Mmmpph!" Arlend tried to shake her 5-year-old voice out of his head. It left when replaced by the sound of trumpets drifting in his window. Arlend felt that his strength had returned to him. He slowly got out of bed and peered out the window, just in time to see loyal royal luggage bearers struggle into the palace. His mother.

Arlend flopped back onto his bed. He had

hoped his father was leaving. He didn't feel like facing anyone right now. And he missed the girl terribly.

'Eggs, tomatoes, lettuce, fruit. Oh, what else did he say? Darn, I must remember. I must!'

Arlend frowned, rubbing his forehead. He was going cuckoo. (This was after frowns. But then again, just about everything is. Adam frowned when he got kicked out of the Garden.) He told himself that he was just hungry after sleeping for nearly a month straight, and that once he got something to eat, he'd be able to think straight. He left his room and went down the hall, sliding down the banister and making his way to the kitchen.

"Arly! You alive!" the cook squealed.

He smiled. "Hello, Shanna."

"Arlend, you feeling better? Does it still hurt? What was the whole matter 'bout your sculpture? Well, well, you can tell me everything later, you must be hungry. Have a seat." She pulled a stool up to the counter for him.

Shanna had been like a second mother to Arlend ever since Meria had taken to traveling everywhere as the Second Lady. Shanna was the only one who understood about his art. And about his favorite foods.

As Arlend ravagingly scarfed down five pizzas of odd toppings, two chickens, a whole pot of clam chowder, a chef salad and a huge marble cake, Shanna filled him in on all the events which had taken place during the month he was out.

"Oh, and your parents havin' a ragin' battle of words over you."

Arlend looked up from licking the icing off a platter. "Over me?" He listened hard. Sure enough, on the other side of the palace, they were shouting. He couldn't make out what they were saying, but it didn't sound pretty.

"Your mother thinks you dead."

Arlend stiffened. In that case, it might be more than just words they were throwing at each other.

"And…oh, Arly, you okay? Why you look so glum?"

"Oh...Uh..." Arlend couldn't keep things from her. He sighed. "I miss her. It was only a day that we really got to be together, but…"

"What? Who?"

Oh. She didn't know what had happened.

Arlend was the only one who took the time to inform this palace servant of things happening in the outside world.

"Well," he started, "so tell me what you know."

"Arlend dear, when I didn't see you at dinner that day, I was a getting' worried. The next day, your father said not to make any for you, that you was probably gonna be out for a while if you was to recover at all. Well I just 'bout had a panic attack right there. Duque said if I didn't take a chill pill soon, he'd have me in the dungeon until - "

"What!" Arlend stood with a stomp.

"Oh, but he didn't, Arly." She motioned for him to sit so she could finish. "Well all's I could do was try to relax an' act like nothin' happened, tried to put things outta my mind by tellin' myself that you was on vacation or somethin' till today when I overheard the words 'Arlend' and 'shockwave' and somethin' about a sculpture of yours. I nearly went up the wall comin' back here, till I saw you, Arly, and oh, I was so relieved!" She threw her arms around him. "But Arlend, you alright now?"

"Yes," he said, informing her about the girl,

the glass castle, and finally, the shockwave. He finished with, "She was everything to me."

Reluctantly, Arlend stood. "Well, I'd better go report to Mother now."

Stepping into the room, Arlend flinched as a cup flew by, barely grazing the tip of his nose before it shattered against the wall.

"It was for his good!" bellowed Arlend's father.

"His good! To kill him, let's see how much good that will do him!" his mother retorted.

"I wasn't aiming for him, dagnabit! And anyway, he's not dead!"

"How would you know?! Not that you would go check on him, no –"

"You think he would want to see me, of all people!"

"Well, you could at least–" And then she saw Arlend. She shrieked, running over and nearly suffocating him.

"You're alive!"

"Good to see you too, Mother," he replied as best he could, barely able to breathe.

"Arlend! Oh, my baby! Are you okay?" She put her hands on his cheeks despite his being taller than her and fully grown.

He smiled warmly. "Yes, Mother, I'm feeling fine now."

She motioned for her son to sit down.

"So, let's try to sort some things out," she said.

"Now that you're not throwing things at me anymore," her husband muttered under his breath.

She pretended not to hear, continuing, "What's happening around here?"

"Nothing," hammered the duque.

"Nothing! You murdered a young girl! I've heard the story! You killed Arlend's girlfriend!"

"Mother," Arlend tried to reason.

"Dear!" announced the duque.

"Why doesn't anyone tell me what's going on?" Meria said, an edge rising in her tone.

"You didn't give me a chance! You –"

"Father, Mother," Arlend cut in. "How about I go get you two some *calming*, green tea, and you can *peacefully* try to express yourselves in a dignified manner?"

His parents, feeling sheepish at having their son intervene, sat down reluctantly and agreed.

As he returned down the hallway with two cups of tea, Arlend could hear them murmuring unhappily from the room at the end.

"No!" his father whispered, just barely within Arlend's earshot. "Nothing of the sort. She looked to be no more than about five years of age!"

"Jovell! What if Arlend has a daughter we don't know about?" his mother said with a frown.

"But Arlend doesn't even *see* women, Meria! When he's not fencing he's always in that…that art studio of his," he said, spitting the last part. There was a pause. "Anyhow, it isn't that big of a deal. You've seen Arlend, he's just fine! He's a young, strong, Highlander, and he's going to get right back to his swordfight competitions and –"

"But what about the girl? What if –"

"Who cares? She was just a girl."

Just then, the couple looked up to see Arlend standing there. He slammed the cups on the table. "Just. A. Girl!" he repeated sternly. "How could you say that? She wasn't just any girl, she was *mine*! I loved her like I would love my own daughter. And what exactly do you mean by 'Who cares'? You might not care, but I was the one who put in hour after hour, year after year on this. I gave to her out of my own life. Ripping her away from me was like tearing out a part of myself! She meant more than the world to me, Father, more than fencing, more–"

"Arlend! That's enough! You are a champion, and fencing is your primary concern and needs your undivided –"

But Arlend was already out of the room. He stormed up the stairs like there was no tomorrow and crashed into his room. Opening the balcony door, he stepped out and climbed onto the railing. He peered to the left, and then to the right. And most importantly, straight down. No one was on the sandy lot behind the palace, five levels below. Arlend jumped.

2
Slave Girl of Etlintas

"Congratulations, you are now my slave!" a voice cackled.

Faylin awoke wondering where she was. She looked around and found herself lying in the backseat of a car parked in front of a large, foreboding manor. (This was after cars.) A grouchy, mid-aged man was looking down at her from the driver's seat.

Suddenly, she remembered. In one, quick, motion, Faylin sprang up and out the door, scampering down the street.

"Hey! Get back here!" He dashed after her. She took a turn in one direction, and then the next. Leaping over objects and ducking into alleyways, Faylin was more speedy and nimble that ever. No more year after year of slavery, no more lifetime of Vizain's cruelty. No more would –

"Faylin!" called the familiar, harsh voice. The girl moaned and turned in her bed to face the wall.

Suddenly, she felt the blanket being yanked off her as the sharp sting of her master's whip grazed her back. Vizain jerked her arm, pulling her off the cot in the tiny, basement cell.

"Why did you sleep so late!" he yelled. "The whole house needs to be cleaned and the yard tended to before I leave for Gosland tomorrow! Get to work!" He shoved her into a wall of the room before storming out.

Faylin sank to the linoleum floor from the impact, but scrambled up hurriedly. Down the hall she speed walked before ascending up the stairs, trying to be fast enough not to get into trouble, but at the same time quiet enough for the same reason. According to her master, nothing she ever did was right. She sighed – freedom was just another dream. Getting a bucket filled with soapy water and a rag, she started on the floor of the grand hall.

"Faster! Faster!" Vizain nudged her with his foot before moving on to the next slave. Keeping a straight face, Faylin groaned inwardly. This was all she had known for the past seven years of her life. Throughout that time, Vizain's sticks and whips had taught Faylin to keep her thoughts and feelings to herself. But worst of all was the bindlet.

The world of Myrada had once been a place of magic and fantasy, but through the years, all supernatural had diminished to superstition; save a few, rare trifles. These remaining inklets of magic were now known as the Seven Wonders of the Ancient World, which may have been a misnomer, since the seventh was just a rumor which had not yet been proven. The enslavement bindlet of Etlintas was the most common of the known six, and was still legal only in Etlintas, though one can find them now and then throughout all the Mainlands.

Many times Faylin's small fingers had pulled at the thin, metal chain which hung loosely around her neck. But it was no use, once this chain was about one's neck, it was there forever to stay. The potency of the thing was really in the charm part of the bindlet, which could be changed from time to time.

The charm was a tiny, oval-shaped metal piece that could open, clasp closed, and of course, attach to the chain. Opened, the inside would bear the master's name, the name of the only person in all Etlintas, plus the whole world of Myrada who could attach or remove that particular charm.

'Are you okay?' It was the Voice. The voice of the one person who Faylin couldn't hide her inner thoughts and feelings from.

'I guess so,' Faylin thought, directing there words toward the one who spoke to her in her thoughts. 'I'll be really glad when all these tasks are finally done and he goes on his trip to Gosland tomorrow.' This person was the only one she felt she could confide in. 'He is so brutal to me!'

'Poor girl. But will you be left outside when he is gone?' Faylin had told this person so much about her life. In fact, she talked to the presence about everything.

'As usual,' she sighed. 'And he will call to me with my bindlet to come back to his house when he returns. If only it were warmer out. Since it's the tenth month, it's winter in Etlintas, which means it'll probably start snowing soon here in Alcott.' As she spoke, Faylin felt a mixture of emotions being emitted, especially when she mentioned Alcott, the capital of Etlintas. She couldn't quite tell what one of the emotions was, though the other was clearly sadness.

'Was that you?' she asked. Sometimes this whole thing caused her to question her sanity. Yet ironically, it was the only thing which kept her going.

'Yes. That was me.'

'Why?' Faylin was concerned, not wanting her only friend to be sad.

'I don't want you to be treated that way.'

She smiled faintly, her emotions being sent on. 'I wish you were in control of how I was treated.'

'Me too. But have hope, I…'

But Faylin couldn't grasp what.

'You what?'

'I…you…'

'I'm sorry, the mindline is getting weak. I can't hear you.'

'I said I…'

Frustration gripped her.

'Never mind. I'll contact you later.'

'You're leaving me?'

'No, I…' Again, she couldn't perceive. 'Look, just trust me. I…'

A slap in the face brought Faylin back to her present situation.

"Did I say you could space out?!" With that, Vizain kicked her (literally) out to do yard work in the back. This was not pleasurable, considering the chilly temperatures. (This was before big, puffy winter coats.) But at least he didn't use the bindlet. Yet.

3
The Voices at Avanaset

Barely pausing as he landed on his feet, Arlend dashed out the palace gates, ignoring the sounding trumpets. Running at a steady pace of 25 miles per hour, he chose the back routes and alleyways of Royaleh to avoid being seen until he was out of town.

Just between the outskirts of this capital city and the rushing, clear waters of the Delythe flowing into the Bulcie was a lush, little grove of trees. Arlend would often come here alone and sit on a boulder, leaning back on the strong trunk of an oak. He'd close his eyes and listen to the birds' sweet melodies and the calming flow of the river.

Here was Arlend's corner of the universe which centuries ago, upon its discovery, was named Avanaset. Here was where the soft voices of the crickets' cheep, the wind's dance, and the waterfall's song comforted him when he was down. Here was where the serene music of nature inspired Arlend's artwork.

But today, all the birds' chirps seemed to lament his loss. A gray, thundering sky hung over head, and Arlend's spirit was dashed upon the stones underneath the river's powerful current.

'Do I really have to go back now?'

Arlend's eyes watered at the sound of her voice, despite its simply being inside his head. He willed it to go away, to stop reminding him of his pain that she was gone, and yet he yearned to hear that voice, that wondrous, beautiful voice once again, for it was all that made him feel the slightest bit close to her. He took a deep breath. No one could understand how he felt about her, or what it was like to be separated from her forever.

'I dread just the thought of getting closer to that place. I want to run, but I'm afraid.'

Suddenly, Arlend came to his senses, as if waking up from sleep. Those weren't random things in his mind, it was his little girl! Arlend jumped up. Why had his father told him she had been killed? Dagnab him, she was alive!

Thunder boomed again as it started to rain. Arlend started heading back to the castle. As soon as the weather cleared up, he would look for her. It didn't matter that everyone would try to stop him; he had no choice but to find her.

'The last kilometer.'

Arlend stopped short. Kilometer? So she was in the Mainlands then. He would need to take a ship. (This was before airplanes.) Arlend quickened his pace. There would be many preparations to make.

Once in his room, Arlend nearly took apart his closet looking for some commoner clothes. After taking a shower, he put on one set and stuffed the only other into his drawstring canvas bag. He knocked on the wall inside his closet. With a slight groan, the wall swung towards him, opening just enough for him to squeeze his fingers into the crack and pull the wall open. Revealed was a safe. Arlend put his thumb on a little circle on the door of the safe, which read his fingerprint and sprang open the door. (This was after fingerprint identification.) Inside were boxes and boxes of coins, both gold and silver, from a lifetime of fencing championships. (Fencing, wrestling, and archery were the Big Deals before baseball, basketball, and American Football.) Arlend removed two square-shaped ones which fit in hand and put them inside his bag.

Concealing everything again, Arlend slung the bag over his shoulder and made his way downstairs to the kitchen to say good-bye to Shanna. He couldn't leave without letting her know where he'd be going, and he was quite hopeful that no one would ask a servant of his whereabouts after they discovered he was missing.

"Arlend! Why you wearing that!" she exclaimed the minute he walked into the kitchen.

"Shanna, she's alive."

"She is? Oh, Arlend –"

"I have to go find her."

"But where?"

"I'm not quite sure," he answered truthfully. "I don't know how long I'm going to be gone. But I have to go find her."

She looked at him in a serious, understanding manner. "I'll miss you, Arly."

He threw his arms around her. "Thanks for understanding. I'll miss you too, Shanna."

They said their farewells, and Arlend went back to his room to take his usual way off the balcony. He made his way behind the central palace down a path toward the royal museum to collect a little something which might come in handy later on. The guard eyed his choice of clothing conspicuously, but said nothing while letting Arlend in.

"I need it for my art," Arlend explained as he walked out with one of the rarer artifacts in the nation. The museum docent was slightly disgruntled but did not dare argue with the marque. Arlend put it in his bag and sauntered off to the wall at the outskirts of the palace grounds.

One of the cats was perched on top of the wall. Arlend wouldn't have minded, but this was no ordinary cat. Intelligent and perfectly fluent in Highlander, the cats which guarded the castle wall were about six feet long from nose to tail-tip. Perhaps the most alarming thing about these cats were the wings sprouting from somewhere below their shoulders. This one was staring straight at Arlend through its large, green eyes.

"Ahem," it said, baring its fangs.

Arlend smiled.

"Why are you climbing the wall?"

The cat left Arlend no doubt of who was in the better position.

"I need the exercise," Arlend replied.

"Hmmm. Really? The wall is higher over there." The cat flicked its tail in the general direction.

"I'm not good enough for that bit."

"Oh. Well then. Do you want me to inform His Highness?"

"No," Arlend said a bit too quickly.

The cat raised an eyebrow.

"Tell him," Arlend stipulated, regaining himself. "Tell him I'm…going for a walk. To find her."

"Who?"

"Her."

The cat was confused. Its first responsibility was to prevent strangers from climbing over and coming in. Well, a stranger was most certainly climbing over, but he was going *out*. Normally, people going out would go through the gate. This was a first. Now, the cat fell back on its second responsibility; to report suspicious behavior to the duque. (Security cameras were probably invented for airports, which were probably invented for airplanes, which they did not have at this time.)

"I will tell His Highness that someone left the castle by climbing the wall so he could go for a walk and find her."

"Thank you."

With a sudden wind from its wide wings, the cat took off. Arlend hoisted himself onto the edge of the wall, and without a backward glance, jumped off.

Arlend put on the Theatre Face, the mask he had taken from the museum and made his way through the crowded street towards the wharf of Glesgow. This Wonder of the ancient world would disguise the wearer's face in a way that looked completely natural, but completely different, the exact look depending on the wearer's wishes. Arlend pictured a man in his mind wouldn't resemble the royal family in any way. The flexible mask formed perfectly to his face. It stretched itself to even cover Arlend's eyelids to form eyeholes through which he could see a ship ahead of him, sitting in the bay. Numerous sailors were loading crates of the Highlanders' well-crafted, fine silver. Arlend worked his way to the port, intending to get on the ship. One of the deck hands stopped him at the gangplank.

"Hey you! What do you think you're doing, eh?" he called out in the common language shared by all the nations of the Mainlands. In his many years, Arlend had managed to gain knowledge of all the languages and geography of the world, and it was finally coming in handy.

"I need a voyage to the Lowlands… I mean the Mainlands," Arlend replied, making the quick switch in dialect and terminology.

"The only way to do that is to help out on deck," the captain said, stepping in.

"You mean, as a sailor, right?"

"It's hard work. Not for the average man." He eyed Arlend from head to toe, looking for signs of laziness.

"I'm no stranger to work."

"You strong?"

"Enough." He fought the urge to smile, for he didn't intend to let on that he was a Highlander.

"You good with knots?"

"I know a few…and learn fast."

"Can you swim?" (Swimming is older than humanity. Because fish are.)

"Yes."

"'Tis bad luck for a sailor to swim, you know. Aw, well. I could always use an extra hand. Understand you won't be gettin' an earning, the trip should be pay enough. Welcome aboard. Oh, and by the way, sailor, what's your name?"

Arlend paused for a bit and said the first thing that came to mind. "Matthew DonPeter." (Highlanders place "Don" in front of the father's name to form the offspring's surname.) He hoped hard they would not ask to see the name on his left hand, a form of identification used all over the world of Myrada.

The captain looked at him.

4

Aboard the Clarabelle

"DonPeter, huh? Funny name. You will address me as Captain Olson and nothing else. Get on board, DonPeter, and meet me good friend John." He motioned to the deckhand who had first spotted Arlend. "He'll teach ye to unfurl the sails. We'll be pullin' up the anchor soon."

Arlend breathed a silent sigh of relief and got on the Nirolfish ship, the *Clarabelle*, where he was soon positioned lowering one of the sails. The wind soon filled it, sending the billowing outward until taunt, and the ship started to move. Out to sea and closer to Faylin, if what he gathered from her thoughts were correct.

On the 4-hour trip from the duque's palace in Royaleh to the port city, Arlend managed to gain a bit of control over the thoughts entering his head from the girl. Now that he was done talking with the captain and the sailor, he let the thoughts flow again, as he gazed out at the sea. He felt her hurting, moaning inwardly as if in pain. He frowned. What was going on?

'Child! Are you okay?' his mind screamed. No reply. Arlend wanted to pound on the thick, glass wall which allowed him to hear her, but that left her without a clue. But there was no wall that he could see, no embodied obstacle he could draw his sword on.

Arlend puzzled over this frustration of his as his work shift ended and he trudged down below deck to find his cabin.

"Is something the matter, sir?" a cabin boy questioned in Nirolfish as Arlend arrived at the bottom of the staircase. "Anything wrong with the cabin?"

"Oh, no, it's alright, thank you," Arlend quickly replied, making the switch between Mainlander to Nirolfish. Right afterward however, he thought, *How weird. If I have just come down the stairs, chances are, I haven't seen the cabin yet. Oh well, he must have mistaken me for one of the customers riding the ship.*

'What is that? Did I hear something?'

"Huh?" said Arlend, aloud in Highlander.

"What was that, sir?" asked the cabin boy.

"Uh, oh, nothing, thanks." Arlend spoke, shaking his head. He kept walking until he found the assigned cabin. *This must be it.*

'What must be it?' came the girl.

Arlend almost jumped. He *did* think, *this must be it, 2B,* but how did she know?

'What is this? Oh, I do fear the beating has driven me to insanity.'

'What beating?' Arlend hurriedly shouted in his head.

'Who are you?'

'Can you hear me?' Nothing.

And then, 'This is quite weird.'

'Child! My little girl! It's me! It's Arlend! Are you alright?'

'What is this? I feel thoughts… Thoughts in my head…that…I'm not thinking…like a voice in my head, but no sound, only *thoughts*, how can this be?'

Arlend let himself into the cabin, trying to recall what he had named her.

'Child?'

'Is someone calling to me?'

'It's me. Arlend.' How he wished that she would

be able to hear him.

'You, who?'

'Arlend, I said.'

'Hello?' A pause. 'Oh. It seems to be gone now. Yet I feel it is still there all the same.'

'I am…well, *here*.'

'Where? And why won't you tell me who you are?'

'I tried, I don't think you can hear me all that well.'

'Oh, I see. Where are you? Are you in my mind?'

'No. But it seems my thoughts are. I am on a ship.'

'Did you say your thoughts are?'

'Yes.'

'Oh, okay. But where are you?'

'Ship. Ocean. Boat. In the sea.'

'Okay, okay, I gotcha.'

Arlend breathed a sigh of relief, shutting the door and sitting down on his bunk.

'Why were you tense earlier?' she asked.

'What?'

'I felt you relax a little.'

'You did?'

'Yes. So you must have been stressed to begin with. Why?'

'I'm really worried about you.' Arlend told her. He wondered how much she would be able to hear him perfectly, the way he could hear her. 'Did you get *beaten*?'

'Well…yes.'

Arlend felt like he'd been slapped across the face. 'Why?!'

'Well…I'm his slave.'

'So what? How dare he.'

'Of course he dares, he's my master. You must not be from around here.'

'Where?'

But she didn't catch that. She continued, 'A master can beat his slave whenever he feels like is, as long as the slave doesn't become extremely injured. As can a mistress.'

'Not if the slave is you,' Arlend grumbled.

'What was that?'

'Tell me where you are. I am coming, and I will beat your master until – '

'Oooh no, don't. You'll get in trouble.'

'Trouble?' He was caught off guard, for back home, if the king and the duque were not involved, then neither was trouble for a marque.

'Vizain is a major political leader.'

'Vizain?'

'My master.'

'Ick, I'd hate to have a name like that…But he deserves it, and much more. What is your name?'

'Faylin.'

Then, it all came back to Arlend. He reflected upon the meaning of that name, nodding.

'What? Did you say something?'

'Nice name.'

She seemed surprised. 'You didn't just say, "Nice name", did you?'

'I did. It has roots in the Ancient Highlander language which was used a long time ago.'

'Wow. That's awesome.'

'You're awesome,' Arlend smiled.

She seemed annoyed. 'Are you being sarcastic?'

Arlend was taken aback. 'No! Of course not,' he thought in shock. 'Why would I be?'

'Well…Because I'm not, I'm stupid and

worthless, and –"

'Who told you that?' Arlend felt hurt.

A pause. 'Vizain…his wife…everyone, really.'

His heart sank. 'Well, you're not. I think you're the most wonderful little girl ever.'

'Awww. You're so sweet. I wish you were real.'

Arlend sighed. 'Faylin.'

'Yes?'

'I love you.'

'What? Sorry, I can't talk now; my master wants me to go clean the bathroom.'

'Will you be alright, Faylin?'

'I…I guess so…' She seemed surprised that anyone would care.

'Do you know who I am?' There was no reply.

For the next week or so, Arlend was consumed with sending thoughts into Faylin's mind whether he was up on deck, in the dining hall, or the cabin. He found that he could choose, whenever, to know what she was thinking, but she perceived only the thoughts which he consciously sent her. And even then, she couldn't always "hear" clearly, as she put it.

'Are you there?' she thought of him one day while he was at work up deck.

'As always.' He smiled.

'Are you still out at sea?'

'Yes.'

'You have been there for quite a while now.'

'Well, I am going across the whole ocean.'

'Where are you going?'

'To find you.'

'To find what?'

'You.'

She didn't quite get it. 'Are you a treasure hunter?'

He chuckled to himself. '…Sure. And you are my treasure.'

'Me? Faylin?'

'Yes, you, my Faylin.'

A pause, before she asked softly, in a curious, yet hesitant manner, 'Why? Why do you even care?'

'I…' Arlend started, but he then squinted. There, about a third of the way to the horizon appeared a sail. It was approaching at a surprising rate from the direction towards which the *Clarabelle* was headed. 'I'll talk later. It seems there is trouble on the horizon.'

'…Okay.'

It wasn't until midmorning that it drew near enough for the captain to use his spyglass. Arlend, of course, had better eyesight than the mortals and didn't need a spyglass. He had looked out before and recognized the Jolly Roger flying on top. He now watched the captain, waiting for a reaction. There was none.

Shielding his eyes, he looked out again. The dagnabed pirates had thrown up a decoy flag, one of a Nirolfish trading ship! But he couldn't warn the captain without giving himself away as a Highlander or even as royalty. Not to mention, the captain probably wouldn't believe him. All he could do was watch the pirates approach the ship and its unsuspecting crew.

It wasn't until the pirates moved outward and made a 180-degree turn and sailed alongside the *Clarabelle* that the crewmen on deck started to notice that something was not right.

"Pirates!" came the shout.

The crew waited tentatively as the pirate ship

approached. They were not terribly scared of pirates, as they had already fought off many pirates before. But their cargo was valuable, one of the most precious to sail the Myradian Ocean, and so the crew were properly trained to protect it. No, the reason they were scared was the flag. It wasn't the flag of a regular buccaneer, but the feared flag of the infamous Captain D'Yunge, scourge of the sea and self-proclaimed king of Arienca and all pirates. They say Captain D'Yunge never lost a swordfight in his life, but Captain Olson had reassured them that this was as much of a myth as man-eating dragons and flying cats.

The crew waited as the pirate ship steadily sailed closer. Every man stood at attention, sword drawn. Every archer perched in the masts, waiting with arrows notched for the command to fire. One of their prize defenses was the huge ballista erected in the center of the deck between the main and mizzen masts. So far, they hadn't gotten a chance to use it, but it performed well in the tests. Now, finally, the crew got to witness its performance for real. As soon as the ship sailed into range, a quiet command was issued for the huge bolt of sudden death to be launched.

The ballista flew through the air and collided with the main mast of the pirate ship, knocking it over. The crew cheered; they got a direct hit! Their ship moved forward in attack to finish off the scurvy pirates.

They were almost broadside now. The archers let loose their arrows, shooting them through the rigging onto the deck of the pirate ship. But the main deck was empty. The order to cease fire was given, and, like some ghost town afloat, the ship drifted eerily until it was broadside. The deck was empty. Not a single soul was aboard.

Behind the sailors, unnoticed by everyone, the pirate crew climbed out of the water onto the other side of the ship. They swung onto the deck, still wet from their underwater swim. Weapons were quietly unsheathed as the pirates crossed from starboard to port without making a single sound. They sneaked behind the sailors, cupped their mouths, and knocked then out with a single blow.

Captain D'Yunge smiled triumphantly as he stared down the length of his sword into the frightened eyes of his opponent, the captain of the ship of their most recent attack. Never had anyone beat him in a sword fight – pirate, captain, man or beast. He called to his crew, who had stood in a ring to watch the fight. They quickly bound the captain up, and carried him unceremoniously below the deck. The Captain D'Yunge returned the cabin he claimed for himself on the ship they'd just captured and sat, staring out across the endless blue waves, polishing his prized sword, and contemplating.

He had risen swiftly from his mysterious beginnings as a lowly deck hand, and now he was almost legend. Some said he was the son of a great king from the Lands Beyond; some went as far as saying he was the son of a god. No one knew for sure. However, his power and reputation were well respected. It was often said among the buccaneers that he had no enemies, save those who were already dead.

D'Yunge liked this mysterious air about him and often used superstition to his advantage. He didn't mind what people said about him, that is, as long as he didn't have competition. The captain's greatest victory was the conquest of Arienca, an island off the shores of Etlintas. On the island he claimed a stone fortress as his own, and promised a safe place for pirates to dock, pick up or drop off supplies, and make repairs on their ships. He set himself up as a king of sorts, the monarch of Arienca and overlord of pirates. Any who resisted his price quickly found themselves in a deadly fencing match against this fabled man, which, of course, they lost. And so he had remained in his kingdom for many prosperous years.

But now things were starting to shift. Whispers spread among the pirate community that this legend was getting old, too old in fact to manage his kingdom. Many young buccaneers saw him as an easy road to success. Surely anyone who bested the fabled Captain D'Yunge would instantly find himself in a position of respect, power, and wealth.

And so D'Yunge took to the seas once more, to prove he hadn't lost his touch. He chose the best crew ever recorded, and set his vicious path through the Myradian Ocean. Yes, the world would most certainly quiver when they hear the infamous Captain D'Yunge had taken to the seas once more!

A knock sounded from the door.

"Cap'n?"

"What ye be wondr'n…" the captain desperately tried to remember the sailor's name, but quickly gave up. "Come in!"

"We searched the galleon, cap'n…"

"And what be inside?"

"Silver, sir! The ship be full of Highlander silver!"

"Silver, you say! Well, order the men to bring it aboard. What a fine way to start a voyage, eh?"

"Aye, cap'n, a fine way to start a voyage!"

Captain D'Yunge sat back in his chair, reassured he was still the best.

Arlend, too, didn't notice the advancing pirates, until one of them smacked his head with the flat of his sword. Arlend cried out, warning the rest of the crew, but the pirate struck out again, this time harder, and Arlend fell to the deck, stunned.

Arlend woke up and looked around. The room was dimly lit, and smelly. But most of all, his head hurt. Arlend raised his hand to rub it. As he did so, a chain came from nowhere and smacked him in the face.

"Ouch!"

He looked around. There were a few feet of chain tying him to the wall. Arlend groaned and started examining. First he noticed he didn't have handcuffs. That was good. Then he examined the chain thickness. They were too thick to break, but all he would need was one weak link, either thinner, or rusted, or aha! There it was! Arlend firmly grabbed the chain around the rusty link and yanked as hard as he could.

Snap! The bond broke. Arlend quickly untangled himself and made for the door with nothing but escape on his mind. He ran head first into a pirate. Arlend didn't lose his nerve for a second.

"May I borrow your sword? Thank you!"

The man was just opening his mouth to reply when Arlend took the sword with his left hand and hit the man with his right, being careful to use only enough strength to knock him out. Arlend tossed his sword into his right hand and ran, taking the steps three at a time. Without pausing for breath, he flung open the door and stepped into the brilliant sunlight. He charged blindly across the deck, blinking hard in the sunlight and flinging his sward wildly to and fro, shouting with all his might.

The first pirate charged from somewhere to his left. He sidestepped his opponent, disarming him in the process. Arlend contemptuously kicked the sword away, while two more approached him. He ducked the first swipe at his neck while parrying the other blow. Soon Arlend was double-armed, keeping five at bay while slowly backing down the deck. Then, suddenly switching tactics, he planted his feet and switched direction, vaulting himself over the heads of his enemies. He ran a short distance, but was stopped by another pirate.

"Gather ye around, boys! Watch yer cap'n handle this son of a biscuit eater!"

Arlend eyed his new opponent. From the boots to the extravagant rags right up to the hat, there was no doubt who was the leader on this ship. Arlend wielded the sword and prepared for this final battle. The rest of the crew formed a circle around the two contestants. The cap'n was happy. It wasn't every day he got a decent match. And this man most certainly *was* a decent match.

The cap'n started with a simple lunge at Arlend's stomach. This one was blocked, but he wasn't concerned. He tried a feint to the right, but at the last second he switched it to a rightward thrust. The prisoner followed his movements perfectly. Now he was attacking, slow at first, and slowly picking up speed. The cap'n followed every thrust, feint, and maneuver with practiced grace. Soon the swords were barely visible, just flashes in the afternoon sunlight. The contestants circled each other, both looking for a weakness, the prisoner desperately looking for a hole in the captain's defense, while the captain himself tried to switch the direction of attack, and save him some face in front of his crew. He needn't have worried, few of the hands could follow the speed of the blade, much less understand the fast sequence and complicated rhythm of this deadly dance.

Then the cap'n saw it, the weakness in the attack. His blade snaked in, and he sent his opponent's blade flying through the air. He pushed his blade tip at the throat of the prisoner. Arlend was beat.

5
Misty Memories

A little girl awoke hazily on a tiny lifeboat in what seemed to be the middle of an ocean. She had no idea where she was. Or what had happened, how she got there. In fact, now that she thought about it, she didn't even know who she was. Or where she was from.

Did she have a family that was worrying about her? Maybe she was the lucky survivor of a shipwreck. The girl continued to scan her surroundings for a sign of something. Anything. Eventually, a ship came into sight.

Wobbling, she stood up on the boat, shouting, "Hey! Over here! Help!" She observed as some people on the deck gathered and pointed. But as it neared, the poor girl realized that it was a pirates' ship. She could do nothing but watch as a rope was thrown down the side and a sailor descended onto the boat she was on and brought her up to the ship.

"Identification," one of them growled at her once she came on board.

She panicked. What was she supposed to do; couldn't they see she didn't have anything with her? But before she even had a chance to hesitate, another dealt her a slap in the face.

"Do what ye be told!" the pirate said, grabbing her hand and examining her palm. Tossing the hand back at her side, he looked up, examining the girl, who cowered under the scrutiny.

"Thar be no origin. Too weak and frail to be worth much."

As they shoved her across the deck, she stole a glance at her palm. What could be so interesting about that? To her surprise, on it was written *Faylin*. She wished she could link that to something. Perhaps the place she was born? The name of someone important to her? But she knew nothing. And her feelings of being lost were not helped by the pirates' rudeness.

They half led her, half carried her down below deck. Before she could react, they fastened her wrists in iron cuffs and locked them. The door slammed shut, leaving her in darkness as they returned to the sunlight. She waited until their rough voices disappeared before allowing herself to cry.

A hand touched her arm. She screamed, pulling away. A tender voice came from the darkness.

"Shhh! They'll hear you." She waited as the girl calmed down. "Hi. My name's Leesha. What's yours?"

"Name? I'm not sure I have one." She now followed Leesha's example by speaking in whispers.

"No name? What is written on your hand?"

She tried hard to recall, before answering, "I don't quite remember, but I'm not even sure it was of any significance anyhow." But Leesha couldn't quite hear what had been said, for there started a great noise on the deck which made their murmurs barely audible. Thinking that the girl had said nothing at all to mean that she truly had no name, Leesha continued:

"Well, I'll have to give you one then…"

Leesha had never named anyone before and was unsure what to do. But she pitied the girl. She probably didn't have a family. Leesha's thoughts turned to her own family, far north of here, before the pirates came. She didn't have any friends, just a dog named…

"Shaylen. Your name is to be Shaylen."

"Faylin," the girl muttered in astonishment. "Well now, I suppose that makes sense…" How did Leesha know? The noise increased.

"I recognize that," breathed Leesha. "It's a fishing dragon. We had them back home."

"A fishing dragon?" Faylin raised her tone just a bit.

"It eats fish. I think it wants to land on the boat." Leesha was using her regular voice now, on the edge of shouting. Still, it kept getting harder to hear.

They listened to the fight above. The boat tipped again, farther this time, then rocked back and forth for some time like a weeble. (This was before weebles were outdated.) Things in the room became loose. A packet of papers fell in Faylin's lap. Without thinking she picked up the first sheet and stuffed it into the pocket of her smock.

Faylin was about to get sick when the rocking stopped. There was one last screech from above, then a mighty cheer from the crew. From her side, Leesha muttered, "Poor dragon. I hope some of those pirates got washed overboard."

The rest of the trip was somewhat uneventful. There turned out to be about a dozen other prisoners. Food came in the form of a tasteless mush each morning in a bowl, which the prisoner's had to share. Sometimes the man who brought it would leave it just out of reach from the stretch of the chain. However, Faylin and Leesha became friends, although Leesha would do most of the talking, and mostly about home.

Once, they stopped on a chaotic island to unload and reload the ship. Upon leaving, they sailed onwards for some time.

It all ended one morning just as Faylin thought she heard seagulls. When the man came down to take away the mush bowl, he brought man with him. The other man carried a whip and a key. (This was before you could open a door by swiping a card of some sort.) With the key he chained all the slaves together, encouraging some with the whip. They were marched out into the sunlight and onto the deck. Faylin tried to stop and blink, but the man forced her to keep moving with a sting from the whip. It wouldn't be her last.

The crew marched them off the deck and down the gangplank, into a busy street. The people hurriedly got out of the pirate's way. They turned their heads and didn't look at the slaves. So they passed through the city, being lead to a large square near the wharf where a man stood on a podium, marketing a young boy off. Then he started rambling off numbers, while people in the crowd would shout and hold up a large wooden plate with a number on it. The boy was handed off to the highest bidder.

Faylin didn't pay too much attention. She was slightly delirious, tired of standing, dehydrated, exhausted and hot. Her vision became blurry. She was roughly lead to the podium, where she tried to look out across the crowd. She stood there longer than most slaves. Feeling faint and out of it, Faylin waited anxiously for the word "SOLD" to be announced, hoping she would somehow be able to get a place to sit and perhaps some cool, refreshing water. However, after awhile she was led off the podium.

"Maybe later," the auctioneer said, shaking his head at her before leaving her alone behind a curtain which hung as a backdrop for the podium, where other slaves were waiting their turn. Relieved for the moment, Faylin tried to sit down, mindless of all else. But instead, she felt herself falling into darkness.

"Congratulations, you are now my slave!" a voice cackled.

Faylin awoke wondering where she was. She looked around and found herself lying in the backseat of a carriage parked in front of a large, foreboding manor. A grouchy, mid-aged man was looking down at her from the driver's seat.

Suddenly, out of the blue, Faylin sprang up and grabbed the handle of the door. Locked.

The man guffawed. "As if that one hasn't been tried! I was hoping you'd be the one to come up with something new. But don't bother now, if you realize what's already around your neck." He winked as enjoyed the look of desperation on her face.

She looked down. She saw nothing more than

what seemed to be a locket necklace, but she dared not tamper with anything. (This was after necklaces.)

He stepped out to stand in front of her door before unlocking it. Roughly grabbing her by the arm, he led his slave into the house where she would be in servitude for life.

6
Pirates

The captain moved his blade for the kill.

"Are you a Highlander?" Arlend suddenly called out in his native tongue.

The cap'n froze and stood speechless for a moment, then slowly, as if out of practice, replied "What?"

"Are you a Highlander?" Arlend repeated, more slowly.

"Why...yes I am. Your...fencing ability is... amazing!" commented the captain, falling back into his native tongue.

"Obviously I still have some to learn."

"No, your improvised sword was too short. You just need a proper blade."

The pirates looked at these two men, both of them equally handsome and imposing, especially now that the unfamiliar one had removed some sort of mask. Once they were fighting as if over the last grain of salt on Myrada, but now they were talking in a strange language, and hugging! The cap'n led the prisoner into his cabin, while the pirates looked onward in complete bewilderment.

"Have a seat," the captain motioned to Arlend once they were in his cabin.

Arlend sat, and shook his head in utter amazement, setting the Theatre Face on the table before them.

"Kaedan!" he exclaimed. "I don't believe my senses!" He had never worn a beard before, and certainly not such a big one. And those clothes! Arlend was completely caught off guard.

Captain Kaedan "D'Yunge" DonJovell chuckled. "Then you're beginning to understand how I feel." He poured them both some rum and sat down. "How are Mother and Father? And the others?"

Arlend sighed, casting his eyes downwards. They would be wondering where he was by now. He pushed that thought out of his mind. He filled his brother in on all that had happened in the centuries since they were teens, after Kaedan had left, shortly after Jovell had become duque. About how their nation had colonized a nearby island, all about the current politics, and about which of their siblings had married which nobles. He paused for a breath before asking, "Why did you leave?"

Kaedan shrugged, awkwardly avoiding eye contact. "It's just… Father. What happened to him. He just wasn't our Daddy anymore, he's Duque."

Arlend nodded sadly. "I understand."

"You do?"

"Well…yes. If you haven't noticed, I'm not exactly where His Highness expects of me to be myself."

This brought a chuckle from the both of them.

"I can't blame you for leaving," Arlend continued. "I'm just glad to see you, after all these years!"

The two long-lost brothers embraced again, which ended when Kaedan said, "So what do you say? Shall we rule the seas side-by-side, mate?"

Arlend laughed, remembering the old times when the two would make-believe to be real pirates with their little wooden swords, with which the game would end with an epic fencing match between the two coming to a draw, and Kaedan would ask Arlend those exact words. (This was before video games.)

Then Arlend spilled about Faylin, concluding with, "I have to go find her. I'd sail with you, but —"

"I understand," Kaedan nodded.

"You do?"

They smiled. Then Kaedan seemed startled all of a sudden.

"What?" came Arlend.

"About a month ago, you say?"

"Yes, about that long."

"Why I saw… No, it couldn't be…"

"What?"

"About five years old, light hair, light skin, blue eyes, with a sort of hesitant but graceful step, you say?"

"…Yes. Why?"

"Well, well, well."

"What?" Arlend was really curious now.

"Well, I'll be… Probably no more than a coincidence, but I saw a girl…I believe it was on the island…" He paused, trying to remember. The wide-eyed, leaning-forward, extra-pressure look on Arlend's face didn't help. But he continued,

"Didn't notice anything special about her, except…
Golly, Arlend, when I laid eyes on her, I could
have sworn I'd seen a sculpture or something of
the sort that looked just like her in your art studio.
But surely…"

Arlend gaped. "Kaedan…" He nodded slowly.
"That's her. That's my girl."

It was Kaedan's turn to be in shock. "You really
did it, Arlend…Will she really live?"

Arlend sighed, looking at his feet. Slowly, he
looked back up at his brother. "I don't know," he
admitted remorsefully.

Kaedan put his arm around his little brother's
shoulder like he would when they were young. "I
hope for you the best. Come, I have something you
might find useful."

Kaedan stood. Arlend followed him through
a passageway and down a flight of stairs to what
seemed to be the lowest deck of the ship. Crewman
walked two and fro, sorting out the loot and loading
the ship with the plunder they had brought from
the other ship.

"Ahoy!" the cap'n called. "Where be me
carpet?"

A rolled up, five-by-three-feet, quilted rug was brought to him. He then led Arlend up to the deck and spread out the Carpet of Judgment.

"I suppose you'll be wanting to take off right away?"

Arlend beamed, realizing what a Wonder was this thing which his brother was about to give him. "Thank you so much, Kaedan." The two embraced with vows to keep in touch this time.

Arlend sat on the carpet. It allowed time for just a quick wave of farewell before shooting out into the sky. As it soared into the air, Arlend held on with a death-tight grip and awaited his judgment. If his motives were pure, he would find a smooth, instant ride straight to his desired destination. But if his conscience was blackened, then he was in for a long, turbulent journey to the place on this planet which would give him the worst. It was a tool used in the ancient world to both award the good and punish the bad, and most of all to judge whether a person was guilty or innocent.

I am not doing this for my own sake, he thought. *My cause is selfless...How can I have a purer motive?* But on his conscience were defying his father and running away. He could only hope his strong wish for all that was good to him would outweigh the necessary wrongs he had committed in order for his true purpose to prevail.

The carpet looped and jerked as it worked its magic. Arlend clung on for dear life as he was tossed about, upside down and twisted around, spun and bounced. He had no idea which direction he was going, or even which way was up! Squeezing his eyes shut, all he could hope was that the judgment would be short and that it would find him innocent.

When it finally stilled to hover peacefully over the ocean, Arlend's stomach felt queasy. The carpet sped up again, but this time, he could barely feel it moving as it rose into the air and swooped full speed toward the horizon. He could not imagine who would want to go through such a trial as that. (This was before roller coasters. Or at least, before people got crazy enough to ride them for fun.) Then again, perhaps his mixture of good and bad had been difficult to judge. Whatever the reason, if it took him to Faylin, it would be worth it all and more.

Something was not right. Arlend had been alive too long for the sullen, unsettled mood hanging over the air of this city to pass under his nose unnoticed. And it became even more apparent when Arlend would try to talk to people in this strange city where the carpet had landed, allowing him to get off before swooping back into the sky where it would stay until it appeared on land again for someone else to find. Greeting a person here was okay, but once his foreign accent showed through, unsettled nearly became alarmed.

"Excuse me! Pardon me!" He tried desperately to get someone, anyone, to stop their scurrying about, up and down the busy streets, to share a few words of help. The only person to even notice was a little boy sitting idly on a bench in front of a shop, munching on an apple. To Arlend, he looked to be about the age Faylin was before he'd lost her. Although, nowadays, everything seemed to remind him of her.

"Excuse me, can you please tell me where I am?" He asked gently to the boy.

"Don't you know where you are, Mister?" he

said with utter curiosity. Here was a grown-up asking him, of all people. And he didn't even make the best marks at school. (This was after school. I can't honestly remember a time before school.)

"Eh…no." Arlend shrugged in a nonchalant manner and continued, as though he were playing a game, "I just got captured by pirates who turned out to be the crew of my long-lost brother; he didn't know the exact name of the place where he let me off the ship." To his surprise, the boy bought it.

"You're the brother of a *real pirate*?" His eyes grew large and round.

"Yep, sure am. And I'll even give you a real doubloon if you help me out a bit." Arlend dug in his pocket for one of the tiny pieces of gold his brother had given him along with the fine sword which was now tied to his waist.

And you should have seen the look on the boy's face. "Anything…"

"Well…Let's start with the basics. What city is this?"

"The city of Rhelni in the land of Lunderint, of course." The boy couldn't *believe* how easy it was.

"What's going on around here? Everyone's so tense."

"You didn't *hear* about the *war*?"

Arlend shook his head, smiling. "I told you. I spent the past few weeks out at sea."

"Oh…right. Well, there's a *really* big war going on 'round here. One of those upper countries. Fighting over land or *something*, I suppose. Mommy says the draft is going to start soon, and *everyone* is worried about themselves or dads or brother or people getting drafted. A *draft* is when people are *forced* to go fight in the war. But *you* don't need to worry, because they don't draft people that are not from around here."

"Oh, that's good." Arlend figured he didn't have spare time to go shoot arrows at people he didn't have anything against over a piece of dirt, although the draft wasn't his greatest concern. War with countries to the north meant he wasn't going to have a good time getting up there to search.

"Well, thanks then." He handed the bit of gold to the kid, who took it eagerly.

"Anytime. For real."

Arlend chuckled.

"You there! Away from my boy!" A rather disgruntled-looking father stopped out from the shop.

Arlend stood to face the man, holding his hand up in apology. "Sorry, sir. I mean no harm to –"

"Foreigner! What are you doing, spy! Police! Police!" he hollered.

"But Daddy!" said the child, grabbing his father's arm. "He's not a spy. He's a *pirate!*"

The man turned white. "Thief! Spy! Gaining on my son! Help, I said!"

"Please, sir, I just – "Arlend protested.

But the townspeople had started to gather around.

Arlend decided the best way to avoid conflict was to slip away that instant. Cautiously, he slipped past another store or two and around the street. Turning another corner, Arlend ducked into a random shop.

He peered out the window to make sure he wasn't being followed. No such luck. The street was starting to fill with common folk, looking this way and that, checking the stores one by one.

Arlend looked around the shop he was in.

Everything in the medium-sized room was a sickening shade of pink: the walls, the carpet, and all the er…goods, if you could call it good; things consisting of puffy, feathery pink pillows, frilly pink dresses, glittery pink high-heeled shoes, and lots of pink jewelry.

"Er, may I help you, sir?" a young lady camouflaged in a pink uniform standing behind the pink counter asked him.

Think fast, Arlend urged himself. Otherwise, there would be yet another person to suspect him.

"Er…I'd. Like. To Buy. A Bracelet. For. Um. My Niece." Arlend spoke slowly, twisting his poor tongue into all the wrong positions to make his words pure and without foreign accent. He figured he'd just hand the bracelet off to Faylin later. *If we both live till then,* he reminded himself, causing a lump to form in his throat.

The shopkeeper raised an eyebrow. "Alriiight." She replied in the same, slow manner. Arlend waited impatiently for the store clerk to give him a bracelet, just any bracelet. Behind him, he watched police run by the window, in every direction. It will only be a matter of time before someone saw him.

"Which bracelet do you want?" asked the clerk for the third time. She was not having the best of days. She had woken up that morning to find that her new puppy, Sweetooth, had found the bread the clerk had wanted to eat for breakfast. She had caught her dog lying next to the remaining fourth of the loaf. Then, later that day, the police had harassed her because of her northern origin, claiming she and her family were spies sent in by the enemy. Her husband had stayed too late at the pub again last night, and wouldn't wake up in the morning. And now, to top everything off, here she was, trying to sell a bracelet to some deaf incompetent.

"Excuse me, sir!" She demanded. "Which bracelet would you like?"

"Oh, sorry…Um…How about this one here?" he pointed to one that caught his eye.

Arlend ran out of the shop and back into the street. He tried to push his way through the crowd. The sooner he was in the open, the sooner he could run.

Just then, he was spotted by the police. Whistles

rang from the streets, and the people backed against the buildings. Arlend ran, turning right. He stopped. There, in front of him, blocking the way were five mounted police, each with a crossbow aimed at him. Arlend tried to turn around, but the route behind him was blocked as well by the pursuing police. He was trapped! Arlend unsheathed his new sword before he realized he had done so.

"Back away!" Arlend shouted. "Let me go, if you value your lives!" he decided to say on the spot. He hadn't planned for a fight, but if that was the only way they'd let him go, a fight was what they'd get.

The police seemed undaunted.

"I am the brother of Captain D'Yunge! If I die, he shall wreck every building in this town, until nothing is left! Back away!" He hoped this threat would convince them. No such luck.

A detachment of the foot police charged, armed with their short blades. Arlend swung around, sword at ready. His blade flickered, feigned, thrust and twisted, but never went for the kill. Each of the ten police lay, either unarmed or out cold.

"I wish no harm!" shouted Arlend. "If you let me through!" And he charged the mounted police. They raised their crossbows in perfect unison, took careful aim, and fired. Arlend sprinted when he heard the twang. He was no longer moving at a sedate ten miles per hour to remain inconspicuous, but at his max, almost 25mph. He shot past the mounts before the police could realize the spy (or was he a pirate?) was no longer moving at a speed humanly possible, but had dashed between their horses, and was now running for his life, down the road and away from the town.

7
The Bindlet

Faylin sighed again, recalling how it had really happened, contrary to her dreams… She would be stuck with the charm engraved with Vizain's name until his death…If he allowed her to live until then. With everyone of consequence being involved in the war, even the most basic slave laws of Etlintas were ignored.

"Girl! Dishes!" Vizain mandated from the dining area. That was how Vizain addressed everyone in the household – "Wife!" or "Son!" or "Butler!" and "Cook!". "Girl!" happened to mean Faylin, who scurried in to clear the dishes from the table to the kitchen sink and wash them. Afterwards came the usual shining and polishing before making the weekly tip to the downtown market. (This was before Wal-Mart.)

Faylin always enjoyed these trips because it meant time away from her master and uninterrupted chats with the Voice. It didn't matter that she sometimes had trouble discerning what it was saying, she loved this faraway (or perhaps imaginary) friend of hers very much, and she would pretend that it loved her back.

But today, the Voice seemed somehow preoccupied. Faylin felt a strange kind of caring and longing sensation, a mixture of affection towards the Voice and a curiosity to know what was filling its mind. She wanted to talk to the Voice, but decided to just let it be. She knew it cared about her, and that was what she needed to know, that someone saw her as more than just a worthless slave girl.

She completed the shopping and arrived back at Vizain's place just in time to gather the scraps leftover from his lunch so she could have a bite to eat. Just as she was finishing up, Vizain kicked her out (quite literally, as expected) to tend the front yard. She shivered in her thin chiffon dress as leaves fluttered in the wind while she got a rake to start on the job.

Meanwhile, Vizain sulked in his room after a most unappetizing meal. Gourmet-style and consisting of some of Etlintas' finest delicacies, for sure, but Vizain was brooding over the war. Just this morning, after a long uphill struggle, he was finally forced to give the word for surrender. The war was over, and Vizain had lost.

Though no food could taste good under those circumstances, Vizain could care less, having whipped the cook soundly. That satisfied him. But then he remembered that he would have to head to Gosland within the week and sign the *@#$%^ peace treaty. This was always the greatest injury to pride. The king was not going to be pleased, but at least that would wait until Vizain returned from Gosland. In any case, the future looked glum.

Vizain hear a soft, small squeak. He looked out the window of his quarters, peering through the bare trees. The gate was open, and the rake abandoned on the sidewalk. *@#$%^! The girl had tried to run again.

Faylin ran. She ran as hard and fast as her short legs would let her. Perhaps this time, she'd escape. Perhaps she could hide. Her feet pelted the sidewalk and spurred her on. She didn't waste time looking around, but something inside her told her she had never made it this far before. Perhaps she could get out of range before Vizain found the master charm. Perhaps the bindlet wouldn't work. Perhaps some divine force was now on her side.

Then, it happened. A sudden, sharp force pulled at her neck, almost choking her. Her feet flew out in front. Faylin's heart lurched as she started falling. She gasped. Her eyelids snapped shut. She kept falling for several seconds. Whippy, thorny branches smacked against her back as though she was tugged. It hit her legs, her back, and her face. She felt as though she was being dragged through a rough, sharp thorn bush, but she was immaterial. She could feel the pierces as the branches, leaves, and thorns tore right through her, but that she had no flesh or bone to stop it from penetrating her all over.

She landed with a hard thump. And opened her eyes. She was lying on her back in the middle of the private parlor with her master glaring down at her.

Whimpering and gasping from the excruciating ordeal, she was yanked up of her feet and tugged outside by her master, who picked up the rake on the way into the back yard.

"Think you can run away from me, you worthless little twerp?!" he said menacingly, throwing her to the ground face-down and positioning the rake a few feet above her.

Faylin fought against her body's aches, urging her limbs to pull her off the ground and away from Vizain and the rake, but her last run had drained her of every ounce of strength.

Vizain started to buffet her with the rake. Again and again he lashed out at her, feeling satisfaction from her cries of agony. "Allow me to remind you," he hollered over the noise, "That you were a poor, unwanted orphan when I spent *my* money to take you in and provide food and shelter out of my pocket. And still you are ungrateful. No one else wanted you, you stupid slug! Anyhow you are small, weak, and don't work up to the two silver I paid for you. I'll show you! Why, you're better off dead!

Faylin yelled like never before. Every shriek that left her lips begged for mercy. All the girl wanted was a chance at life, though life itself was of little prospect to her. She had no memories prior to being on a boat in the middle of the ocean at the age of five, but now she supposed she really had been abandoned. Tiny, weak, and useless, as the one who took care of her never let her forget. Unwanted, and left to die, she was sure of it now. *Perhaps,* she thought as her mind began to fog, *I'll just be doing the world a favor by dying.*

8
Stop It

All was well at the Arbol Inn on the main street in Alcott, Etlintas. The huge war involving nearly all the coastal Mainland nations had just ended. Many were enjoying a relaxed, happy breakfast on their way home at the breakfast bar of this inn. The coffee was toasty and warm, like the sunshine pouring in the large windows. The aroma of freshly baked pastries filled the air, and cereals of all sorts lined the counters. Everyone was refreshed and content, quietly enjoying a hearty meal. And then —

BANG.

Arlend pounded his fist on the table in frustration. This got him some peculiar looks from the others enjoying an otherwise tranquil breakfast, but he could have cared less. Six years had gone by. Six years! And he still didn't have a good lead as to where she was. Arlend shook his head. He would try asking Faylin again.

Connecting to the mindline, Arlend felt that

something was bothering her. 'Are you okay?' he wondered.

'I guess so,' Faylin thought back. 'I'll be really glad when all these tasks are finally done and he goes on his trip to Gosland tomorrow.'

So Vizain is going on a trip. Arlend thought to himself.

'Yes. He is so brutal to me!' Faylin thought to him.

'Poor girl,' Arlend thought sadly. 'But will you be left outside when he is gone?' Faylin had told this person so much about her life. In fact, she talked to the presence about everything.

'As usual,' she sighed. 'And he will call to me with my bindlet to come back to his house when he returns. If only it were warmer out. Since it's the tenth month, it's winter in Etlintas, which means it'll probably start snowing soon here in Alcott.'

Arlend's mouthful of milk and cereal spewed across the table as he coughed and hacked. This caused some heads to turn, but Arlend was already out the door and down the block by the time anyone had a chance to start wondering what the matter was.

'Was that you?'

Arlend could feel through the mindline that she meant the sadness he was feeling earlier over her present situation, she did not catch the sudden change in his emotions.

'Yes. That was me.'

'Why?' he felt her wonder.

'I don't want you to be treated that way.'

He could sense the warmth she felt inside as he said that, and the warmth radiated to his own heart to know that he had made her feel this way despite her harsh life, a warmth that made the normally immune Arlend completely unaware of the chilling winds as he ran down the street. She was in Alcott! He couldn't believe his luck and how close she was this whole time!

'I wish you were in control of how I am treated,' she thought.

'Me too,' he thought back. 'But have hope, I am coming for you, Faylin!'

'You what?'

'I have found you! I am coming for you right now! You will see me today; think of it, dear Faylin, today!'

A slight pause. 'I'm sorry, the mindline is getting weak. I can't hear you.'

'I said I'm coming. *Now.* Which street does this Vizain of yours live on?'

He could feel her getting extremely frustrated from not being able to get what he had said.

'Never mind,' he told her. 'I'll contact you later.'

'You're leaving me?'

'No, I'm going to focus on other ways of finding you. Look, just trust me. I will *find* you, alright Faylin? Then we'll talk in person.' He felt no sense of comprehension being made in her mind. He gasped. He could feel she was in pain. Sadly, he supposed he shouldn't distract her from whatever duty her master (how he felt hatred and envy towards that word!) assigned her, for his worst fear was that she would be hurt.

Now he completely concentrated his thoughts on locating her. Six long years he had searched the world, and he was finally right here, in the very city where she dwelled! And he concentrated. Hard. Not on thinking *to* her, but *about* her. Arlend thought of her eyes, her smile, all about her, especially all that she meant to him… He took a shockwave for her, and he would go through all the pain again gladly, if to save her from harm, he would do *anything* for her…

Suddenly, as he had so longingly hoped, it clicked. He gradually started to shift his thoughts to where she might be, and the mindline undertook a metamorphosis to a whole new dimension. He could faintly sense her now. Somewhere on the other side of the city… to the south.

Nothing could stop him now; he would not rest until she was once again in his arms. *This time,* he thought as he ran down the street in the general direction, *to stay.*

A couple hours later and at the other end of town, Arlend dashed down the alley, the excitement rising as he could feel the mindline get stronger and stronger. He could feel her. Any minute now, he would see the beauty he'd been longing for so much.

Suddenly, the thoughts stopped and her voice became audible, clearly coming from his right, a high-pitched, terrified shrill. Arlend had no choice but to scramble up the fence to his right. In a rushing frenzy, he fell off into some bushes within the yard.

Healing and gathering himself together, he crouched and peered though the leaves. Across the yard lay the pure magnificence, just as he had seen her brilliance last…Even the same size as he had last seen her. But this was no time to ponder growth; a fierce-looking squat figure was beating her mercilessly with a rake. It was all Arlend could do to keep himself from rushing up and tackling the government official full force and wringing his grubby neck. He had to plan this out.

Vizain took out all his anger and stress on the little worm which lay at his feet. A blow for the stupid war. A harder blow for losing it. And for having to face –

Suddenly, the grin was wiped off from his face.

"STOP IT."

He looked up to see a man, about a head taller than himself, wielding a sword.

"Excuse me, sir?" came a voice so soft and

quivering it surprised himself. His mind went blank. As he urged himself to think, the rake was swiftly taken from his unsuspecting hand and tossed aside. Just a pair of terrified eyes dared to move to see that the rake had gone clear over the fence! This was no ordinary soldier the general dealt with. Vizain ate his pride and took to the opposite direction. But before he could pick his pace up, he felt something brush against his ankle. He saw the ground come towards him as he face-planted on the only patch of cement in his otherwise grassy yard. He turned over only to find the sword at his throat.

The giraffe-like man said through gritted teeth, "Remove the bindlet."

Vizain cleared his throat. "No…never." His voice shook. "She's my slave."

"You name the price, I'll buy her from you," he paused. "Or, I could kill you instead."

"Okay, okay! Girl, come over here." He expected the girl to approach hesitantly as usual, but she didn't. How dare she disobey. "I said, Girl! Get over –"

"Idiot," growled the man with the sword. "You'll be lucky if she's still alive by now, with all that you –"

"I could care less whether she's alive, she's a slave, she's –"

"You'd better care, your life's at stake!" Arlend was surprised by his own boldness. But kindness had never mattered while Vizain owned Faylin, so Arlend could not be expected to show him kindness in return.

"Heh heh…I-I'll go fetch her then," he croaked sheepishly.

"NO. Don't touch her! Ever again!" Arlend marched over to where she lay. Blood had trickled from her torn skin onto the ground around her. Her eyes were closed. Her form lay completely still.

9
Father Duque

"He WHAT?!?!" roared the duque, stamping to a standing position off his throne.

The flying cat, though a good six feet away, took a step back. It swallowed and tried to explain as best it could.

"Sire, one man tried to come in, but left when told he needed a key."

The king grunted indifferently. Typical.

"The other was going out, and – "

"WAS IT OR WAS IT NOT ARLEND?"

"I-I'm not quite s-sure, your highness, I'm not very good with faces, you know," stammered the cat. He could almost see the smoke blasting out of the duque's ears.

"AND WHAT DID HE SAY?"

"S-simply that he was going for a w-walk, your majesty." It gulped before choking out, "To find h-her."

"HER?!" he bellowed.

"Th-that's all the man said, Duque." The cat's

wings fell limp down its shoulders apologetically.

The duque sunk back onto his throne, burying his head in his hands. *What have I done now?*

The cat flicked its tail nervously.

"Dismissed," came the muffled voice of an exasperated duque.

Full of relief, the cat gave a rather rushed, clumsy bow before scampering out the large doors of the throne room.

"Frederic…" moaned Jovell. There was no reply. "FREDERIC!"

In rushed the secretary. He swooped into a bow. "Yes, sire?"

"Summon the General of Criminal Justice and cancel all my appointments for today."

"B-but you have a meeting with the king, your highness."

Jovell pounded the arm of his throne with a clenched fist. *Dagnab. The king needs to die so I can become king, and then there will be no one who can overrule my decisions.* He immediately wished he hadn't thought that, and admonished himself for such an evil thing, making his outraged mood worsen.

"Whatever. Summon the General of Justice, I said!" The secretary was hurriedly heading out the door when the duque suddenly shouted, "HALT!"

The secretary snapped around to face him. "Yes, sire?"

"Don't summon him. Just tell him to send his best search party for my son." A simple search-and-rescue team would not be sufficient to bring someone with Arlend's strength anywhere.

"It will be done, your majesty." The secretary bowed and made a hasty exit. Minutes later, the general appeared in the doorway. His large strides brought his toughly-built self to the foot of the throne quite quickly, where he knelt.

"I thought I didn't summon you!"

"My deepest apologies, sire, I-"

"Why are you here then!"

"If it pleases you, sire, I –"

"NO! Nothing pleases me right now. Just spit it out."

"Which son do you wish –"

"Which son do you think? Look around, who's missing?"

"Uh…er…" the general was at a loss for

words.

"ARLEND, of course!"

He was taken aback. "Arlend, sire? Has he not been missing for a month now?"

"NO! He died and then ran away! Just go find him and bring him here!"

A rather confused general turned and walked away briskly.

Jovell felt that perhaps he should correct his slip of the tongue. "HALT!" On the other hand, it was too much of a hassle. "Hurry up and find him!" he repeated, not knowing what else to say. Upon leaving, the poor general feared that either he, the duque, or both, were seriously losing it.

Jovell stood in his royal chambers preparingfor the meeting with the king when a soft tap was heard at the door. Nobody dared knock on the door of his private chambers except for the younger of his own children, coming to seek Meria.

"Mommy's not in here," he called.

"I want to see *you,* Daddy, please?" A small, sweet voice pleaded.

Jovell sighed and opened the door. "Your father

is busy, Rosie, can –"

"Daddy, just this once? *Please*?" The youngest of the DonJovell children, Rosie stood just below Jovell's waistline. Her bloodshot eyes and puffy cheeks said she had been crying more than just a little, and inside, all she wanted was to sit in her daddy's lap and be told that she was loved.

Jovell looked down at this child with mixed feelings of care and annoyance. *This is Meria's job,* he thought, unmindful of each little girl's special need for her daddy. But deep down inside, he knew little Rosie deserved at least this much from him; for she was the only to have been born after Jovell had become duque. The only one to have never known what it was like to have a dad that wasn't constantly busying about running a country, without a moment to spare.

Feeling reluctant, yet guilty all the same, Jovell let the girl in. Strangely, he felt as though he'd almost forgotten how, as he knelt on one knee to meet her eye level. Then he stared at the carpet, not knowing what to say. But there wasn't a need, for Rosie threw her arms around him. "I love you, Daddy," she squeaked.

And then something clicked inside him, just to hear those words. It had been so long since he had heard them, not to mention, accompanied with an unconditional embrace. He had long since forgotten what it meant to have a relationship with his children, to play with them, and simply be there and not just a workaholic sharing a roof with them. As he basked in his daughter's arms, he wondered if Arlend felt the same kind of joy and satisfaction as Jovell felt now to hold his doll or whatever it was in his arms.

Then he remembered. He hadn't given Arlend a chance. Jovell had tried to destroy her that very day. He was overcome with guilt, hoping that Arlend wouldn't have felt the same way about her as Jovell cared for his children.

He wondered what had happened to the girl after Arlend had fainted and Jovell, out of desperation, had her put in a boat and pushed out to sea. If it really was alive, would it still be by now? And where? Now he wondered whether Arlend would be willing to give up the search. Would he be willing to search the whole world for her?

10
Charming

Just as Faylin thought it was all going to be over, the beating stopped. She heard some livid voices arguing. Her head throbbed, making the voices sound distant. She felt herself being lifted up by strong and warm arms as she faded out.

Faylin awoke to the sounds of birds softly singing and rushing water nearby. She could sense someone holding her, and she felt comfortable. Something inside her allowed her to trust this person, as she breathed in a scent that seemed distantly familiar, as though from a dream or past life. The being radiated a strange sort of warmth that started on the parts of her skin which were touching the person and spread throughout her whole body. All the pain and hurt left her gradually, until she felt more comfortable and safe than ever before.

She breathed deeply, feeling that she must be in some glorious afterlife, being held by an angel. But what if she were only unconscious? She dared not open her eyes. But she had always wanted to see what an angel looked like. She finally decided she would let her eyelids barely open to form thin slits. *That way,* she thought, *If I'm not in the afterlife and Vizain is still there, then I will still be sleep enough to let this dream continue.*

She was surprised when she was met with a face looking down at her that belonged to neither Vizain nor a glowing spirit. Startled, she blinked and started, wide-eyed. There was definitely something special about this man who was gazing at her with concern written across his face, though she couldn't say what.

"Oh! Faylin! Child!" he whispered, clutching her close to him and brushing his lips against her cheek. "Are you alright?" There was something about the way he spoke which resonated in her heart. She recognized the voice as the one which had been quarreling with Vizain as she drifted off. But there was something more, something deep, and strange, yet that felt good. Maybe it was how he genuinely cared about her while…No one else did…But the Voice. The Voice! Something about this man connected somehow. Ah – they used the same words with her, in the same, loving manner with which no one else ever spoke to her with.

"Do I know you?" Faylin asked.

The man looked at her, first surprised, and then replied excitedly, "Yes! I am the voices in your head, the one who has searched for you for years, who tried to save you in the swamp, and – "

"You're a real person!" she cut in, exclaiming. Mixed feelings flooded her mind. Part of her was unpleasantly shocked, for she had told this person everything, and he was a real person now! But that couldn't suppress the overwhelming joy she felt, for the only one in the world who gave her the friendship and love she longed for truly existed.

Arlend, on the other hand, was slightly taken aback. "Yes…I am a real person. You don't remember me?" he asked dejectedly. "I'm Arlend."

Something about that name rang a bell inside her. She searched her mind for what it could mean, but came up empty. Perhaps those five years she had lost from her memory…

"Child," he asked, trying to change the topic.

"You didn't tell me you could heal like a Highlander. Before, when Vizain would…"

She looked up at him with a puzzled expression on her face. "What?"

"You…you healed yourself. How?"

"I…I didn't. You healed me."

Arlend was puzzled. Yes, he had wished she would get better, but no one could heal others, only Highlanders could heal themselves. He gathered from talking with Faylin on the mindline for seven years that she had somehow become like a mortal Mainlander – she couldn't run fast, see far, or heal quickly.

Then Arlend remembered something. He handed her a folded and crinkled piece of paper. "This fell out of your pocket."

Faylin took it. "Oh, thanks."

"What is it?"

Faylin unfolded it to show him.

"It's a map…but why is everything disproportional…Oh! This is a Highlander's map!"

Faylin said, "There's some writing on the top, but I can't read it. Can you?"

Arlend looked at her. "You know how to read Highlander, don't you?"

"Yes...I've always known how. I'm not supposed to know how to read any language though, not to mention the one from the mysterious Lands Beyond across the ocean."

"Faylin, it's alright. You're not a slave anymore. See?" He motioned to the chain around her neck.

She looked down. She had been uncharmed; all that was left now was a bare chain. She looked back at him in wonder.

Arlend smiled. "I bought you from Vizain. You're free."

She embraced him again. "Then I belong to you now."

"You have always been mine," he laughed. "But I will not have you enslaved to me."

"Come, there's something we must do." She took his hand and led him through the park to the other side, toward the street.

"Where are we going?"

"You'll see. So, what does the map say?" She laughed, "Quite honestly, I've tried to read it, though I shouldn't. I've read lots of things, actually, but…Well, the print's just too fine." Arlend watched her walk and talk. Her step was light and she was merrier than he had ever seen.

"Let's see…" He held his hand out, and she placed the map in it. He looked. On the coastline there was writing on both sides. One side was just the cartographer's name, an M. Oolman, but on the other side… "The key is three", he mumbled. "What does that mean?" He figured he could puzzle over it later.

"Fay?...Oh, and is it alright if I call you 'Fay' every now and then?"

"Of course! You own me; you can call me whatever you want."

He shook his head. What had that demon disguised as a man taught her? "No, Faylin. Do you want me to?"

She thought about it. "Sure." She decided she really liked the idea. The only nicknames she'd had were "Girl" or "Dungbeetle" or "Worm". She liked the way "Fay" sounded, and it made her feel close to Arlend, which he immediately guessed.

Soon, the two were walking around in downtown Alcott. Passing by a jeweler's, Arlend was reminded of the bracelet he had purchased for her. He opened his bag and fished for the bracelet. When he glanced up again, Faylin was nowhere to be seen.

"Faylin!" He turned around frantically. "Faylin!" he dashed down the street wildly, searching this way and that. He poked his head in a random store and shouted, "Girl. This tall. Blonde. You seen her? Seen her where?" He tripped over his Etlintian words like a blind man running through a forest.

All he got was shopkeepers sadly shaking their heads. One more person for their tax dollars to feed at the mental institute. (This was before taxes. Taxes were even before school.)

Arlend himself felt he was going crazy. He had just found her; he might as well roll over and die than lose her now!

'Don't say that! I'm not worth *that* much. How much did Vizain charge for me anyway?'

'Faylin! Where are you!'

'Over here.'

'WHAT!'

'Relax, I'm in the jeweler's, right where you left me, remember?'

'Are you alright? Are you hurt? Did –"

'Relax, it's okay. I'm buying something here.'

Arlend ran like there was no tomorrow to the jeweler's. He burst in, and upon seeing her sitting on a tall stool facing the counter, he shouted furiously, "Faylin! Don't do that to me! You nearly had me worried sick! How could you run off like that?!"

Faylin kept her cool, as she was simply used to people shouting at her in a less than patient way. She calmly hopped off the stool with a little, wrapped box in her hand, looked up at him, and said softly, "It was you who ran off. Besides, you could have just asked me. It's not like I'm going to run away from you."

"Faylin! Somebody could have abducted you and –"

"Weelll," she said sweetly. "That's why I got you this." She handed him the box and smiled in a way that melted Arlend's heart.

He avoided meeting her eye as he sheepishly unwrapped the gift. He stared blankly at it. In the box were two charms engraved with his name, one had a clasp on it. "Oh, Fay…" he breathed, shaking his head. "I can't use this." He looked at her. He got down on one knee so they were level.

She put her little hands on his shoulders. "I want you to have it anyway."

He looked down at it again.

"If you don't," she said, "then someone else might. It'd be easy, since I am uncharmed."

"Alright…" he agreed. He took hold of the charm with the clasp and held it up to her chain, charming her. To his surprise, the clasp changed before his eyes so that the opening disappeared to leave a single piece of metal completely enclosed around the chain. He was taken aback; Vizain's charm did not look like that.

"It's a permanent one," Faylin explained. Then she teased, "Sorry. You can't sell me anymore."

Arlend was wordless. He threw his arms around her. "I love you, Faylin. I'm sorry I yelled at you. I was just so worried…"

"It's okay," she said hugging him back. "Oh," she remembered. "One more thing. You have to hold your charm in the hand which has your name written on it, since you're the only one who can use it. When you use it, think of –"

"Stop," he said softly. "Don't."

"What's wrong?"

"Look," he shook his head. "I told you, I'm not going to use it. Ever. And that's a promise. I charmed you only so that no one else can. I'm never going to order you around, or hit you, or…" he shrugged, searching for the right words.

Faylin embraced him once again. "Thank you. I love you, too, Arly. And I'm going to call you Arly, not Master, ok?"

He laughed. "Great."

11
Really Real

For supper that night, Arlend took Faylin out to eat at a fancy diner she'd only heard of before. As the waitress walked off after Arlend helped Faylin order, he admitted to her, "I am so glad to finally have you with me again."

Faylin beamed. She was curious about what he meant by "again", but mostly she was just happy. She often kept her head bent and eyes downcast as was customary for slaves, but she now looked up to meet his eyes.

She took all of him in – his strong, yet soft, deep-set hazel eyes, the shape of his nose, and the short beard that ran from his wind-tussled hair to his chin. She wanted to remember every minute detail about this person who she secretly imagined as the father she'd never had, so that if she woke up from this glorious, sweet dream, he would always be in her memory.

Arlend happened to accidentally wonder what she was thinking at the moment. He was slightly taken aback at that he found. He tried to hide his shock, but Faylin didn't fail to notice the fleeting look of bewilderment which crossed his face for a split second.

He knows! She thought. Her head dropped lower than he'd ever seen as her eyes fell to her lap in embarrassment. *I can't help it. It's just too good to be true.* She hoped he wasn't hurt by it. The last thing she wanted was to disappoint him. She'd even rather go back to Vizain than hurt this man who'd given her everything and who she cared for more than anything.

"No, Fay," he murmured, leaning across the table and brushing her cheek softly with his hand and gently lifting her chin a bit. "I'm not hurt. It's alright. I understand; you just need a little time to adjust."

She blinked, stealing a glance at him before returning her eyes to their prior, downcast position.

"Take as long as you need." He whispered tenderly. And he thought, half to himself, yet also making it audible to her mind, 'If good memories are what you want, then I will fill your days with things which will be worth remembering for a lifetime… For as long as it takes for you to realize this really is meant to be.'

When the food was set before them, Arlend dug right in. Faylin simply sat there, watching him.

Arlend looked up. "Aren't you hungry?"

She nodded. "I'm waiting for you to finish."

He gazed at her incredulously, at a loss for words, and set his fork down. "Eat with me, Fay," he uttered softly, an invitation rather than a command. "You're not my slave."

She tentatively reached out for her silverware. Arlend lingered till she had taken a bite before touching his food again.

Faylin savored the warm, rich taste of her chicken. She had never had food like this in her life. She finished every last bit of her meal and raspberry cobbler dessert. She opened her mouth to say something, and then closed it again. But Arlend already knew what she wanted. He held his arms out. She crawled into his lap and rested her little head on his chest. He wrapped one arm around her, absent mindedly fingering his charm that was on her chain. It wasn't a plain, metallic charm like most others. Embedded in the center of the shiny, silver oval was a white piece with dried flowers pressed on by a thin cover of glass. Two pink flowers, one on each side of the sky blue one, were pressed into the shape of tiny hearts.

Faylin's eyelids drooped, shifting her gaze downward to his hand. Her arms formed a tight grasp around her hero as though holding him tight would prevent her from ever losing him. 'Now that you're so close, I could never bear to have you leave me...please don't...' she begged in her thoughts, too exhausted from the day's many events to speak.

'Never,' he mentally assured her while touching his lips to her forehead.

'I don't see why you would do all this for me. Why me?' she wondered as her eyes fell shut all the way, allowing her to drift into a deep, peaceful sleep like never before.

A subtle smile played at Arlend's lips to see her so calm, so still, yet so... alive. How he had come to miss those dazzling eyes, that angelic face, that musical voice... 'Perhaps someday, you'll know,' he thought to the soundly sleeping child. After paying the bill, Arlend carried Faylin to his hotel room and tucked her into the bed.

Going to the hotel lobby, he located a janitor who lent him a hammer. The concrete just behind the hotel was fit for the task, so Arlend chose a spot and took out the master charm of the bindlet. Putting it on the moonlit ground, Arlend wielded the hammer and brought it down on the detestable object of enslavement. With Arlend's strength, just the effort of a soft tap destroyed it once and for all. He scooped up what pieces he could and stuffed it into his pocket.

'Now you're truly free,' he whispered silently to the precious figure asleep on his bed when he returned to his room. He flipped the lights off and sank into a chair for some shut-eye himself.

The weather was simply splendid the next morning, so Arlend decided to take Faylin to a beach just north of the Dazzel. The two took a ferry down the river.

Cheerful sunlight poured in through the leaves above the path they took through the forest.

Birdsongs echoed through the warm air, the place being very temperate compared to Alcott. The oaks and elms soon gave way to palm trees.

"Wow," Faylin breathed at the sight of what lay before them, without another person in sight.

The sun's shining rays danced off the musical waves. Little pebbles and pieces of shell dotted the fine sand. The ocean's magnificence stretched as far as the eye could see to where it met the sky on the horizon.

Energized by the place's splendor, Faylin flew into a sprint towards the water. She ran in a carefree, joyous way, a perfect reminder to Arlend of –

"Be careful!" he shouted as he saw Faylin fearlessly dash into the ocean. Before he could break into an actual run, he was already at her side in the water, ready to catch her should there be a rock to trip her or a sudden drop beneath. She grinned, slipping her tiny fingers in his hand. Just the bit of concern he showed towards her that she'd never seen anyone else show made her feel almost significant.

Arlend inhaled, taking in the majesty of their

surroundings, made complete with her company. He thought of how this place was so tranquil, yet so full of life in a way which reminded him of Avanaset, only this was much larger. Just like the joy in his heart was greatly multiplied by being in this place, because Faylin was with him. In his mind, Arlend toyed with the idea of how the name "Faylin Avanaset DonArlend" would sound.

Arlend reached into his pocket for what was left of the mutilated charm. He turned and tossed the bits out in the air, letting the wind carry it over the water.

Faylin put her hand in the cool, spring water and formed a scoop with her hand, lightly tossing some of the liquid at Arlend. He twirled around.

She tensed. Was this allowed?

A smile played at Arlend's lips. His flat palm smacked the water, sending quite a spray in Faylin's general direction. She flinched, giggling as she became soaked from the shoulders down. Soon, the two were splashing and laughing, chasing each around.

Faylin was stepping back to dodge one of Arlend's wet ambushes when she felt her foot slip on something. She had barely started falling when Arlend immediately caught her up in his arms.

She clutched him tightly. She wasn't sure what surprised her more, the sudden plunge, or Arlend's inhumanly swift reaction. Arlend chuckled under his breath. "Are you alright?" he questioned.

She nodded.

Deciding it was about time for a rest, he carried her to a grassy area a few yards from the tide line, sitting down and setting her in his lap in one, fluid motion.

"What was that you threw into the water?" Faylin asked.

Arlend shrugged. "Watch this," he challenged, bending down and picking up a stone from the ground. He held it out in his palm for her to see, and then clenched his hand into a fist. Faylin watched in awe as a grinding noise was heard. When Arlend unclamped his fingers again, the rock had been pulverized to dust and was now indistinguishable from the substance he had tossed into the ocean earlier. Faylin gaped. Arlend grinned.

"So…everything I've heard about the Lands Beyond and its people is true?"

Arlend laughed. "You didn't believe me?"

Faylin flushed. She hadn't believed *in* him completely.

Swinging one arm around his neck, Faylin reached out and gently ran her little fingers on his face. He was so real, and yet too good to be true. But in that moment, it dawned on her that her simple mind could never conjure something as great as this, reaching beyond her wildest imaginings to materialize depth that she couldn't even fathom. And that was what his love was to her – deeper than she could understand. Although he was too good to be true, he was much, much too good to be just made up.

She put her head on his shoulder and hugged him. "It really is you. You're really real," she breathed, feeling herself being filled with an inexpressible joy.

12
Back Across the Ocean

Gunther fell to a slumped heap among the shrubbery dotting the beach just to the north of Balzac. It had been a hard, tiresome, and worst of all, fruitless six years of searching. After a long internal struggle for the past few weeks, Gunther had finally given up. Perhaps instead he should be the first to set foot on a different planet. Instead of forming his own army by creating intelligent life to take over the world, perhaps he could go to Marzo to capture an army. He could –

Gunther sat upright all of a sudden. There, walking along the beach were two figures. Gunther lay back down. "You are going crazy," he announced, not half to himself, but to himself alone. "You're just hallucinating. Ha. Ha," he teased. "Gunther is a crazy head, a crazy head, a crazy head," he sang with an off-pitched croak.

The two figures walked by, chatting merrily with each other, oblivious of him.

Gunther sat up. This was no laughing matter

now; he was either coming down with a bad case of schizophrenia or going up into the stars with luck. He scratched his head and weighed the possibilities with his options.

1) He could go interact with them, and they would disappear upon closeness or touch, proving Gunther's insanity.

2) He could go interact with them, and they would most certainly be real, proving Gunther's luck had taken a change for the better, no, the best! And success would be his.

3) Upon interaction, they could prove most certainly real to Gunther, but in all reality, were not.

The third possibility had Gunther absolutely stumped. What if they were real, but really weren't? Meaning, what if they were real to Gunther, but really weren't real? Meaning, unreal to…the rest of the world…But did majority belief define reality? What *was* reality? Whatever it was, Gunther had long since lost touch with it…Just like he'd isolated himself from the rest of the world.

Perhaps reality meant something different for each individual. Perhaps reality was simply... Whatever one believed it to be. And the belief would create the fact...Reality. Whatever one held to be true would simply be his or her reality. *So we create our own realities,* Gunther thought. *Truly, I have a dizzying intellect.*

So Gunther decidedly followed the figures, preparing for confrontation. If they were real to him, what did it matter what the rest of the world thought? Believing in his success was what would *make* his success.

A little ways down the beach, little Faylin giggled. Arlend beamed: It was worth all the trouble in the world to see her, to touch her, to hold her, and to be the one to make her laugh.

He picked her up, and as they came in contact, he was filled with new strength, and he swung her around in a circle before carrying her close to him. She squealed with delight and wrapped her tiny arms around his shoulders.

In the past several weeks, they had traveled

south along the oceanside, and as Arlend looked into her eyes, he knew that nothing short of a piece of heaven had fallen down on him. Here he was, walking on golden sand, listening to nature's heartbeat in the waves embracing the beach.

"Such glorious thoughts," her cute voice said teasingly.

'Ah, but the best thing of all is that you are with me, my heartlight,' he thought at her.

She leaned her head against his. "Arlend," she wondered aloud. "What is a heartlight? And…why do you care so much about me anyway?"

"Faylin, I –"

"SIR!" A scraggly man fell to his knees before Arlend, nearly tripping him. "I implore you; take your servant with you where you will go!"

Arlend looked at him, stunned for a moment. "Ah…Just about to cross the ocean, actually." *That should lose him for sure. Who is this maniac?*

"AH, so am I, Master."

"Oh good, I assume you have arranged your transportation already?"

"Yes, on whatever transport you shall take, I shall board to serve, Mas –"

"*Regrettably,*" Arlend emphasized. "It is already booked full." He side-stepped the man, walking by him.

"SIR!" he begged, appearing again in front, to Arlend's annoyance. "Even if I have to hide in your suitcase –"

"That's full too."

"Or sail in a lifeboat tied to the ship –"

"There won't be any."

"Or hang on to the railing –"

"You'll fall off. Sorry," Arlend tried to sound apologetic, but it just didn't work.

"Or hide –"

"Look," he orated, trying his best to be patient to the mental cripple. "I'm building a boat for two, so there won't be –"

"I will take the heavier part of the manual labor, Master, and obey your every bidding so that the building and journey will be much faster," he pleaded. And added, "Your wish is my command, Master, I –"

"First of all, stop calling me that." Arlend figured it couldn't hurt, having an extra pair of hands to help him do the building and rowing.

And anyhow, Arlend would watch his every move. "Secondly, go cut some wood."

He bowed lowly before Arlend. "My greatest thanks to you, Mas –uh, sir."

But it was not as Arlend thought it would be. Barely hours into the building, the man began to grumble.

"The wood's too hard to chop, sir. Just too hard to chop."

"Sharpen the ax then."

A little while later, he returned from sharpening the ax, saying, "This ax is too old to sharpen."

"No, it's not," Arlend told him.

And a bit after that, "This ax is too strong to sharpen."

"No."

"This ax is too dull to sharpen!"

Arlend sighed. "Then go gather enough provisions for our trip."

He picked up the ax and chopped more wood in minutes than the man, Gunther, as he said his name was, had produced in the past few hours. When he looked up, Gunther had returned with a brown and a banana. (A brown is an orange which has turned brown. And this was long after browns.)

Arlend took Faylin by the hand and headed to the supermarket with Gunther tagging along.

"Well?" he asked Gunther as he and Faylin were done buying everything the two would need for the long trip back across the ocean. "What are you going to eat for the next 32 days?" It wasn't until then that Gunther started filling a basket with provisions. Arlend shook his head. Then, to Arlend's further dismay, he handed the basket to Arlend, who said, "What?"

The man looked at his feet. "I don't have money."

Arlend held the basket out to give it back to him. "Look, I'm sorry. I don't think you should come on the journey after all, I –"

"SIR! I beg you! My wife and children starve at my home in Lavalle, I must return in order to make a living and support them! Sir, please, I –"

"How could you leave them like that in the first place?"

Gunther thought for a moment. "I-I thought I would be able to find a better job here." And then quickly added, "But I was wrong."

Arlend was suspicious. He asked in the Lavallean dialect of the Highlander language, "Do you swear that is really the truth?" Lavalle was an island off the shore of the Highlands, its mother country.

"I do, I assure you, good sir," he replied in flawless Lavallean.

Arlend had to agree, and paid for the food. The three went back to the beach to finish building the boat.

"This piece of wood is too splintering to touch!"

"Here," said Faylin. "Hold it right here, on this side. There you go."

"Aheh heh." Gunther looked around, hoping Arlend didn't catch what had just happened.

Arlend was looking directly at them. He turned away, smirking at seeing the little girl showing Gunther how to get the task done.

"My arms are sore!" Gunther declared after ten minutes of rowing. Taking a day of rest after finishing the boat, they had set sail at sunrise. The weather was perfect and there was even a breeze in the right direction.

"How are you going to get a job if you can't do any work?" Arlend asked, trying to keep the annoyance from his voice.

Gunther frowned and kept at it...for another five minutes. "Ugh! How many hours has it been?"

"Arly, can I have a turn?"

"Are you sure you want to, Fay? It's apparently harder than it looks," he said, glowering at Gunther, who nodded vigorously.

Faylin, who was clearly accustomed to work, put in a good 15 minutes at almost the same speed they were going when Gunther had been rowing. It wasn't until Arlend insisted on it that she took a break.

They continued on like this, with Gunther complaining incessantly, Faylin trying to help in whatever way she could, and Arlend doing most of the work. That was, while trying to get Gunther to do more work and Faylin not to overwork herself the way she had been raised.

Finally, one day at sunset, land came into

Arlend's view. Excitedly, he took Faylin's hand and pointed with the other. "See that over there?" But she didn't.

"What?" asked Gunther.

"Land!" Arlend proclaimed. Gunther looked hard, but didn't see anything. "Highlanders," he mumbled under his breath. "Always getting excited too soon."

"Do you have something against Highlanders?" Arlend glared at him. He was getting rather crabby with Gunther by then, and was looking forward to reaching the Lavallean shore and being rid of him.

"Uh, no, not at all, I was –"

"You were brought this far, this fast by us Highlanders," Arlend lectured. Faylin was about to ask, "Us Highlanders?", but Arlend continued, "And allow me to kindly remind you that had it not been for us, you'd still be begging on the beach."

When the boat was just several hundred feet from the harbor of Quasheba, the capital of Lavalle, Arlend found that for the first time that month, his sandals were untied. Faylin was crunching on the oars with great fervor, and when Gunther saw Arlend reach for his shoes, he offered to tie them for Arlend. Surprised, Arlend let him.

Then Gunther stood up on the boat. "Land! It is land, my homeland! My –"

Arlend shouted over the ruckus, "Sit down! Or you'll –"

But it was too late, the boat tipped, sending the three into the water. Right off, Arlend reached for Faylin, for the water was still well over 200 feet deep. He realized his two shoes had somehow been tied together, and in a very tight knot at that. Arlend scrambled in a panicked frenzy, which caused bubbles in the water to surround him and deter his vision.

He felt for the laces. Just as he thought he couldn't hold his breath any longer, the knot came untied. He kicked his sandals off and pushed to the surface for a breath of air before going under to search for Faylin. He turned this way and swam that way, but neither of the two was seen. He poked his head above the surface again. He heard a scream come from the harbor. Wiping the seawater from his eyes, he saw Gunther running off carrying a kicking and screaming Faylin.

Arlend swam for the harbor, cursing Gunther under his breath. What did the fool think he was doing?! Arlend wished he'd never shown him pity or brought him along. Scrambling onto the nearest beach, Arlend sprinted after them, ignoring the sharp stones beneath his bare feet. Despite the fact that a police officer stood leaning on a fence by the side of the road, Gunther shoved a driver out of his carriage, climbed in, and took the reins. Bother Arlend and the policeman, who snapped to attention, ran from opposite sides of the road towards the hijacked vehicle, colliding into each other.

"Sorry, sir, Arlend said hastily, scrambling up.

"You'd better be. Not so fast!" the officer shouted as Arlend turned to go.

"I truly apologize, Officer, I really haven't time to lose, see –"

He was replied with a whack in the face from the policeman's billy club. Arlend, who had not seen that coming, was knocked to the ground.

"You are not dismissed until I say you are, slug!"

Arlend, slightly dizzy from the blow in the head, looked up to see a few more policemen gather around, all with their billy clubs out. Arlend groaned as they all started hitting him, rambling on about submitting to authority and whatnot. Authority! Arlend remembered: he was no longer in the Mainlands, he was in Lavalle.

Arlend fought the pain, healed the bruises, and stood, drawing his sword. He swung around in a circular motion, chopping all the clubs to stubs.

"As Arlend DonJovell, Marque of the Highlands, I command you to stop immediately!"

The police blanked for a moment, before shouting, "Imposter!" and "Arrest him now!"

Arlend was a bit baffled and out of practice, so what had become a group of eight soldiers handcuffed him just as he was starting to struggle. Now the carriage was nowhere in sight, and Arlend knew Gunther hadn't been doing something mindless, he'd kidnapped Faylin.

"Look at my identifica –" he protested.

Someone dealt him a slap in the face, quieting him.

"There's no need, we know how you fakers

can make gloves, burn and tattoo, and more," said another.

"Taking advantage of the duque's being in town, are we?" a third asked him.

"Well, then, why don't we just take this hooligan to the duque and let him deal with it himself?"

Arlend's ears perked. His father was in town? And they were taking Arlend to him? It was too easy. All he would have to do was sit back, wait for his father to announce that it really was Arlend, his son…But wait. Faylin had first been separated from him because of his father. There was no way he'd let him search for her again. Besides, his father might try to kill her again. At any rate, he would probably never see her again.

Arlend felt his world crash down around him as they led him away. He didn't protest or struggle as all, Arlend felt as though there was nothing left to live for now.

After walking for what seemed like ages to Arlend, the officer who was chosen by the rest to find out where in the city the duque had gone returned to report they were going in the right direction, and the duque indeed still planned to arrive at the house on the hill within the hour.

Meanwhile, Gunther, despite the girl's screams, knew nothing of what was going on anywhere except inside his own head. He had finally gotten hold of her and managed to lose the marque.

The hollers turned into sobs of "Let me go! Take me back to Arlend!" and as Gunther strapped her down to the dissection table, her tears turned into pleas, all of which Gunther ignored. This was the moment he'd been waiting for. This was when he'd discover the secret to intelligent life. He contemplated how he should best take this thing apart. After pondering for a bit, he decided on using a gag to silence her, and after that, he made the cut and started draining out her blood.

Gunther cackled, thinking of how he'd *finally* accomplished this feat, since making his plans one morning six years ago.

13
Now That's News

Connor whistled a tune to himself as he went about his morning paper route. He liked the little place he was in, on the outskirts of the bustling city of Quasheba. It was peacefully away from all the noise of the metropolis, yet within range of all the major necessities.

"Top 'o the morning!" greeted a well-aged man tending to his garden on this sunny, clear day.

"A good morning to you, too, Sir." Connor handed him the Quasheba Daily Post. (This was before news went online.)

"Thatta boy. Fine weather we're a having today, eh?"

"Sure is."

He headed on to the elderly woman knitting on the front porch of the next house down.

"You can just set that down right there, young lad." She spoke gently as he gave her a nod and put the paper on a little wicker table near the door.

Departing from there, the paperboy realized

with reluctance that he had reached the end of the road. Only one house was left, the one he always stalled to do last: The house on top of the hill. Keeping his head bent and pace quick, Connor ducked into the alleyway. Sandwiched between two streets, the hill was several houses long itself and about two stories tall at its highest point, just wide enough to accommodate the single, large, old house built there.

Rumors dictated that a mad scientist lived alone there, meddling with uncanny concoctions which would cause the eerie sounds that were heard faintly every now and then. Others secretly believed he was a wizard, gathering the poor and innocent small creatures which dwelled among the trees dotting the hill to cast strange and terrible spells upon them.

Children of the suburb would play games of witches and ghouls of the haunted house while their parents condemned it as a blemish of their otherwise perfect neighborhood. Though it was all too visible to the inhabitants of the surrounding abodes, no one ever went up to the house on the hill. Even the postman hardly went there, for whoever – or whatever – lived up there did not make connections with the rest of the world.

And then there was Connor. The only dreaded part of his whole route was going up to the hill. And once there, the boy dared not get near to the house. Hurling the paper towards the front door of the house, he turned and hurried for the foot of the hill just in time to hear a huge explosion take place right behind him.

Wood cracked and glass shattered following a rather loud *Ka-BOOM* as a voice cackled from inside, "IT WORKED!!!" Neighbors turned and shook their heads, then went back to whatever they were doing. Connor dared to steal a glance behind him before scrambling down the bottom of the hill. Most of the windows were gone. Oily black smoke rolled out of each one.

Then the door opened. Out from the smoke stepped a middle-aged man. He had unruly hair and off-green protection goggles. His lab coat was splattered with all sorts of unidentifiable substances to the point where it was near impossible to discern its original color.

"Heh heh heh," he guffawed insanely as he

fetched the newspaper, a few feet away from the doorstep for which it was aimed. Going in, he slammed the door behind him, causing more bits of glass to fall.

Once inside, Gunther sat down at the table in the kitchen which had been transformed into the laboratory of a madman. He poured himself a cup of tea and began to read the morning paper. All was quiet and calm and just right for a bit of relaxing news. Gunther shuffled past the latest on bombings, the war in the Lowlands, and the most recent brutal murders... No, those were a slight bit *too* relaxing. And then, a headline caught his eye:

Insanity Infests Royal Court

Now *that* was news. Reading on, it seemed to Gunther that on the bay of the Highlands, Lavalle's mother nation, quite a spectacle had occurred involving swords, guns, and blasters of enormous amounts of deadly energy with the Duque and his son on opposing sides. But the real intriguing thing was…No, it *couldn't* be.

Gunther pulled out the Spectacles of Knowledge which he had bribed off a friend of his in the Lavallean legislature. This Wonder allowed the user to read in between the lines. Literally, words appeared between the lines of the text in the paper as Gunther put the glasses on. Sometimes, the words would read, "Truth, this is truth, truth it is" in repetition. Or sometimes, the opposite would occur, and the words would read, "This is fraud, it's a lie, trust it not", over and over again in each line. Sometimes, the reader would get *really* lucky and there would be extra information in between the lines. This was what happened when Gunther donned the glasses. Not only did he see the words "This is truth" embedded in bold repetitiously, a fainter, nearly transparent set of words ran over it.

Gunther nearly drooled over the paper as his eyes devoured this news. Twenty long years he had labored to discover the secret of life. Twenty long years, and not a hint of getting anywhere close. Bankrupt, friendless, and long gone eccentric, this was just what he needed to complete his long, hard research. But thanks to a certain someone, he would have to experiment around blindly and endlessly no longer. He'd simply "borrow" the sacred mystery from someone else...

The trip from Lavalle had been a long one. Gunther had booked his voyage immediately and left two days later. The journey to Glesgow lasted another three days, then he had to *hike* to Royaleh! There were no carriages or horses for that matter. (This was before taxis and Rent-A-Car. And Gunther did not own a car.) So Gunther did the unspeakable: he walked. All the way from the port to the capital. He estimated (quite incorrectly) he must have walked over a hundred miles each day. So it wasn't until a whole week had passed since hearing the news when Gunther arrived at his destination.

Boldly entering the city of Royaleh, Gunther proceeded straight down the center of Main Street. Ah, the joyous bustle of civilization! How he had come to miss it! No more would he stay out of a metropolis.

Arriving at the gates of the palace grounds, he knocked on the door. Nothing. He knocked again. Then he heard a voice from overhead.

"Perhaps you should use your key."

Gunther looked up. He rubbed his eyes in astonishment at the creature which loomed above before looking again. No, it couldn't be... A *cat*! With *wings*! Gunther had never heard of anything of the sort. A talking, flying *CAT*! Gunther blinked hard. The beast, which must have weighed nearly 120 pounds, did not go away.

"It's okay," the cat continued. "I'm sure no one will hurt you if you let yourself in."

"I don't have a key," Gunther replied.

"Well, then, I guess you can't go in. Only those with a key can go in."

"I'm a visitor!" Gunther exclaimed. "Can't you let me in?"

"No. I'm only a guard. Only humans have keys. I guess you'll have to ask a human with a key if you want in."

"Where could I find such a human?"

"Inside, I guess."

Gunther shook his head in exasperation. Perhaps he should try the swamp. Or just go home. Ah, but he had traced this for his whole life. He could not give up now. He'd just have to search.

News always popped up in one way or another.

A paper boy brought Gunther back to earth. He was waving the paper in his face, calling out, and "Two pennies! Extra, extra!" as loudly as he could. Gunther bought a paper just to get rid of him. There, on the front page, bold letters gave the claim, 'Young Marque Goes Out to Sea'. He put on the spectacles.

"Aha! Brilliant!" Gunther started back to Glesgow.

14
Xetimorphicansic Acid

The scenes of her life flashed through Arlend's mind, especially the scenes which were shared with him. Thoughts of "Why? WHY?" pounded in his head with every beat of his heavy heart. He didn't notice much about where he was led, except he noticed they went up a grassy hill.

Soon, they stopped in front of a door which had been bashed and broken. The police shoved the unresisting Arlend through the door. The other followed into what seemed an abandoned mess. There was a single chair by a run-down table covered with multicolored stains. Rats scurried about as flies feasted on molding food. There was a great stench about the place, and struck Arlend as the place in the worst condition he'd ever seen. Windows were shattered, the whole floor creaked. Arlend reminded himself that he could care less of his whereabouts, his life was over.

"I guess we just wait here for the duque to arrive."

"Why would he come to a place like this?"

"Beats me."

Amidst the hushed discussion of the officers, Arlend could hear Faylin crying in his mind. While he relished being able to have a bit of her somehow, it tore him to hear her cry like that.

Then he remembered the mindline. Perhaps... would it still work? He'd forgotten about it in their past month or so spent together. He had never counting on something as wretched as this to happen.

'Arlend! Arlend!' he could hear her now.

'Child, I'm sorry,' he said. He meant those words more than he ever had as he used what he hoped was the mindline. 'There's nothing I can do. I am so, so sorry.'

'The bindlet! Just use it!'

'...I'm sorry. The day I made that promise to you...Faylin, I destroyed the charm. Faylin, I love you,' he cried.

'I...I love you too,' her thoughts faded.

'Faylin? Are you alright? Faylin!'

Nothing.

Then, the trumpets sounded.

Arlend turned away. He did not want to face his father. He heard the sound of footsteps entering.

The Lavallean officers stood to greet their superior counterparts from the Highlands. Then the duque stepped out from the group clustered at the ramshackle doorway. The Lavallean group bowed. One stepped forward.

"Your highness, we have here an imposter claiming to be a marque."

"Arlend?"

"Well, uh…" the officer turned speechlessly to the others. "Who did he claim he was?"

But the duque had already walked towards the figure in handcuffs sulking in a corner. He put a hand on his shoulder. "Arlend."

He shrugged off the hand, in the process, inadvertently allowing the duque to see just enough of his face to recognize that it was him.

"Arlend, look. I owe you an apology."

The Lavalleans glanced at one another nervously. It couldn't be! They had not just arrested a marque dressed as a commoner.

"But," the duque continued. "I'll give it to you later. The man who has her is a lunatic who thinks he can take her apart and –"

Arlend looked at him. "What?"

The duque snapped the handcuffs to pieces. "I've come to this house to arrest him. We'd better hurry."

He motioned towards a flight of stairs which all the soldiers took, following Arlend.

If Arlend had ever thought the place he'd just been in was the worst place ever, that was because he'd never seen the basement of it. Off-colored bits of glass and stinking substances were spread across the whole floor. The only furnishing in the place, which had walls smashed down in order to make it one, large room, were counters and tables, all of which matched the floor, only they were piled with bottles, beakers, and strange instruments which one would never find in a scientific laboratory.

Arlend's heart nearly stopped when he laid eyes upon a table at the center of the room. On it was Faylin. She lay strapped down, unconscious, and deathly pale. The worst thing was the tubes. She had tubes poking into her flesh in several different places. The tubes had a dark maroon interior, as if blood had been drained through them, but there was no more.

"Ah, you have come to say good-bye?" a sinister, yet familiar voice snickered from behind. Too familiar. Arlend turned around.

"Gunther." Arlend's voice came harder than stone, colder than ice. In that one word, he summed up for all the words which he could not say, for words could not describe the anger and hatred he felt.

"You go see to the girl, I'll take care of him," stated the duque.

Arlend moved –

"Ah ah ah! Not so fast. You don't go near her."

"I'D LIKE TO SEE YOU TRY TO STOP ME!" Arlend bellowed so loudly the glassware on the counters trembled in fear.

Gunther held up a corked bottle in his hand, ready to project it towards Arlend. The bottle enclosed a greenish liquid.

"What, a bottle of pickle juice? Is that the best you've got?" Arlend moved towards Faylin.

"Xfetimorphikansic acid," Gunther declared

coolly.

Arlend whirled around to face him again, for Gunther alleged to hold one of the only poisons deadly to Highlanders. If the bottle broke, and even a drop of the acid touched his skin, he would become weak in minutes. Even the scent of it could cause a Highlander to dizzy and faint.

From the corner of his eye, he saw his father motion to the soldiers to advance quietly near Gunther and for Arlend to keep Gunther distracted. What if it was really a decoy, and the duque had come to arrest Gunther for some national offense, and was just borrowing Arlend's help? Could Arlend ever trust his father with matters concerning Faylin again? Arlend decided he had no choice but to take his chances, and distract the maniac.

"How do I know that isn't really pickle juice?"

"You want to smell it?" he smiled.

"What I want to smell is your dead body roasting on a spit!" Arlend was amazed that he could say such a thing. He quieted his conscience. He knew that if anyone deserved it, Gunther was the man. "For all I did for you. For all *she* did for you. And THIS IS HOW YOU REPAY US?!And where are you wife and children, did you kill them for what little love they could force themselves to give you? You –"

"Aaaaaaagh!" His father's men grabbed Gunther from behind.

Arlend rushed towards Faylin as the bottle flew into the air. All the soldiers scrambled to get away from the falling object. But as Arlend hurried to unbind Faylin and carry her to the door, he saw that his father held on to the murderer, despite the risk of his life. The bottle landed and shattered, its outward drops barely missing the duque by hairs.

"Quick!" he shouted. "Arrest and evacuate!" The duque's orders were swiftly carried out, though there was a shuffle as everyone tried to squeeze up the stairs while keeping the flailing and cursing Gunther subdued.

As those around him held their breaths, Arlend checked Faylin for signs of life. She had no pulse.

15
One Heart, One Blood

"Height?

"41 inches."

"Weight?"

"35 pounds."

"Age?"

Everyone had managed to get out safely, and the squad escorted Gunther to the place where he would be detained until they took him to the Highlands for his trial. Arlend was checking Faylin into the E.R. while doctors tended to her.

"What do you think?" he asked softly. "Based on her stature."

"She's in the average range for a five year old."

Just then, a nurse walked up to them. "Sir, she's suffering from severe hypovolemic shock."

Arlend tried to recall what that meant…Oh; she was dying from blood loss. "Can't you replace the blood?"

"We could try, though the chance would be

extremely slim. Her body has already shut down."

"What is her blood type?" another nurse came in and questioned.

"C," Arlend muttered with a faraway look in his eye.

"Sir? We need to know her blood type right now if there's to be any possibility of survival at all."

"It is C."

"Sir, her *blood type,* please."

He looked directly at her. "I said, her blood type is C."

"Sir!" She shook her head. "He's going out the window," she said to the others. "Please think about this very carefully. If you answer incorrectly, she *will die*. Is her *blood type* A, B, AB, or O? And while you're at it, is the Rh factor positive or negative?"

Arlend frowned. Just then, the duque walked in. Everyone stood and either bowed or curtsied.

"That's my son you're talking to. Listen to him."

They were found dumbstruck, and all muttered apologies. But among themselves, they wondered:

"Type C?"

"How can it be?"

"Must be a Highlander thing."

They looked around, but the marque was nowhere to be seen. In the commotion, Arlend had sneaked into the intensive care unit.

"Sir?"

Arlend looked up. A nurse stood at the doorway to Faylin's room.

"I truly apologize. We don't have any donations of type C blood."

"I'll give it."

"But sir…It's too great of an amount."

"Nothing is too great for me to give so that she can live."

"But sir, you would most likely die."

He took a deep breath. "That's a risk I'm willing to take."

After much debate and convincing everyone, especially his father, that it was what he truly wanted, more than anything else, Arlend signed a stack of papers, and it was done. Ounce after ounce they drew from Arlend.

"Son, you can still back out at any time if –"

"No, Father. This is really what I want to do."

"Well…I guess you are old enough to make your own decisions now, my boy." He sighed. "I would help you, but –"

"I know. I've got the rare Rh negative, which she also has. Thank you so much for everything, Father. You have no idea how much I appreciate this."

The duque smiled. "It was the least I could do, having caused you so much trouble and pain. The both of you." After a pause, he said, "Son…How did she get your blood?"

Just then, Faylin's eyes blinked open. "Arly!" was the first thing she said. Though butterflies danced in Arlend's heart to see that she was going to be okay, all he had the strength for was to manage a weak smile and say, "I'm so glad you're alright," in a soft voice, barely above a whisper.

She turned to the duque. "What's wrong with Arly?"

The duque sadly shook his head. He wasn't sure he should alarm her with the news, right after she awakened. But Arlend nodded, she had the right to know. So the duque calmly and slowly explained to the girl what Arlend had chosen to do, and despite his being strong, he probably wouldn't be able to heal himself this time.

Tears rolled down her cheeks. "Arly, *why?*"

"I love you," he whispered.

"But Arly…why me? Arly –"

"Shhhh." He motioned to be moved closer to Fay's bed where all the tubes once again brought his blood to her. He would tell her the story, her story, no, *their* story if it was the last thing he ever did.

16

The Seventh Wonder

To his disappointment, Arlend was awakened from a sweet dream. *The* sweet dream, the one sweet dream he didn't like having, for he would always wake up to find that it was not real. And yet he longed for the dream, just to feel her presence for a little, precious while. Now that his mind was on the matter, he had to go see her. Of course she was not real…. But when he was alone with his work of art, he could let his imagination run wild.

Arlend got up from bed quickly and made his way towards the palace's art studio. Truthfully, it was simply his, for no one else in the Highlands gave much of a care for creativity. To his dismay, he was cut off by the duque along the way.

"A good morning, Father! Lovely weather we are having today!" He walked on, hoping to bypass the ruler.

"In a hurry to trump the others, are we? Well now, come tell your father about your latest victories." The duque smiled.

Arlend sighed. Why did it always have to be about fencing, wrestling, racing, and being tops in the nation? Day after day, for Highlanders who never had to work for the food, it was all they did. Surely, there had to be more to life.

Seeing the look of dismay on his face, the ruler said, "Alright, alright, I know you're eager to get out there. Tell you what, I'll just come watch."

Don't get me wrong now, Arlend loved his father dearly. And it wasn't every day that the duque would leave his work to watch just for one man. But despite Arlend's being well over full-grown, the two just still didn't see eye to eye.

Trumpets sounded as they left the royal premises. Any commoner would have relished in the honor of walking out with the ruler so ceremoniously, but Arlend's heart was back in his workshop.

"En garde!"

Arlend and his opponent struck their swords so hard that, had it been in this world, claps of thunder would have been heard as they dueled with lightning speed. Arlend advanced with the forward thrust with such force that his opponent stumbled back a step. His opponent feigned a stab to the left and speedily averted to the right. But Arlend's reflexes and agility in the block was one of the many things which made him among the best in the Highlands. Unprepared for such a swift comeback, the fighter hesitated for a split second. Long enough for Arlend to knock the sword from his hand.

Those who stood by cheered, some shouting Arlend's name. But the fight was not this marque's game. Next came a ladies' event. Seizing his chance, Arlend slipped away from the outdoor arena. Speeding in the direction of the palace at nearly 20 miles per hour, Arlend easily could have won the races, which were to come soon, had he ever had the motivation to do so. He never went over 17 miles per hour at most in competition, making him an average runner to the rest of his world. But as for this moment, what Arlend raced toward was no thing which the rest chased after; gold, fame, and pride. He was headed to the one place where he truly found himself the most, his art studio.

Hardly even short of breath, Arlend burst

into his workshop with his sword still tied to his waist. There it was, the accomplishment which truly took his breath away. The masterpiece. *His* masterpiece.

Her 5-year-old, ceramic figure stood still, like time frozen in a perfect moment. Her feet barely connected to her stand as she held the position of being forever mid-step in a carefree and fun-filled run; the look of eternal, pure joy solidified on her face. Years and years of hard work and dedication had Arlend put into this creation. From crushing flower petals into paints to get just the right shade to straining at accentuating every detail, the word "passion" fell short of describing how he felt towards this work of art.

He reached out and held her cool, tiny hand in his. Her skin was pale like a starlit path, graced by rosy cheeks. Oceans were the artist's favorite sight, and it was no surprise that her graceful lids framed eyes the color of sea as he ran his fingers over her sandy hair, like sunlight reflecting off a golden beach. Since conceiving the idea all the way through the process and yesterday's victorious completion, Arlend would imagine what it would be like to talk to her, to laugh with her, to…

A soft tap was heard at the door. "Master Arlend?" called a voice.

Arlend sighed. He hated being interrupted in times like this. "What is it?" He inquired in a tired tone of voice.

"A delivery for you, sir."

Maybe this didn't have to be so bad. Arlend sauntered over to open the door. One of the palace attendants handed him a cardboard box which appeared to have been brought in the mail.

"Thanks," Arlend muttered, shutting the door again. He looked at the shipping label. It was addressed from a George C. Quincy. Arlend recalled the name as belonging to a man who had wrote to the marque two days ago claiming that he had discovered the seventh Wonder of the ancient world. "Lifedust," he had called it. Upon reading the letter, Arlend had shaken his head. He had heard better. Nonetheless, he ordered a sample as he did with each of these letters, which he received on a regular basis. Arlend enjoyed seeing (and laughing about) what crazed inventors could come up with in a desperate attempt to get attention from a marque and the general public.

Some of them were actually somewhat eye-catching, including a *very* pretty diamond that lit up on its own at night, a paintbrush which could produce different colors of paint on its own depending on the force you used... Others were not as impressive, like the horn which claimed that when blown, would get the attention of anyone the user wanted within a mile radius. The loud and horrible noise it made had more or less gotten *everyone's* attention within that radius, that is, in the form of complaints. The servant which Arlend had tried to summon complained of a headache and left. (This was before aspirin.) And then there were ones which were simply too far out. Like a bottle of water claiming to be from the fountain of youth (It might as well have been tap water for all the difference it made to a Highlander) and a lamp claiming to be able to summon a genie when rubbed. (It exploded. Produced were two lawsuits and no genie.)

Arlend tore open the package to find a oddly-shaped glass bottle with a white, glittering mist swirling within and a tiny slip of paper. That was odd; he typically received pages and pages narrating epic (and often, far-fetched) tales of how the item was "discovered" and how they wished to be honored for such a feat. This slip of paper simply read: *"Use with caution, as this is the only portion within our world. Arrange 49 candles in a heart formation. Place 3-7 drops blood into container. Close lips tightly around opening. Blow and release"*. That was sure weird. Arlend put the jar and the slip of paper aside, unsure whether it was worth a try.

That night Arlend lay in bed, the events of the long day going through his head. The fencing tournament had gone well, he thought. He got first place, but that wasn't anything new. Then his thoughts drifted to the "lifedust". He found himself considerably curious about what the stuff in the bottle could do.

Finally, Arlend fell into a night full of broken fits of sleep. He dreamed of his sculpture again. And about the lifedust. A million different possibilities and scenarios of what it could do played themselves out in his slumber. Finally, Arlend couldn't stand it any longer. He rolled out of bed and pulled a tack off his bulletin board. It was still dark, and so Arlend tiptoed silently all about the castle searching high and low. The sun was starting to peek its shining face over the horizon when he finally came up with the number the instructions called for.

Ambling to his workshop, Arlend started arranging the candles. It was not an easy task considering the size of the room (or rather, the amount of items piled everywhere), but there was just enough empty space for them if he went around his sculpture, encircling his masterpiece within it. But when he stood back to look at it, the shape was off. Arlend arranged and rearranged, and finally decided that one could clearly tell it was a heart.

He picked up the bottle from the windowsill where it was left the day before. The sunrise cast a magnificent radiance on the glittering, white mist which had not ceased its swirling motion inside the container.

Arlend took a deep breath and popped the cork off the top. He set the bottle on the windowsill and held his left thumb over the round opening, pricking it with the tack in his right hand. His blood dripped into the substance. Instantly, the white vapor began to swirl faster, now with a subtle hint of a soft pink. Arlend rubbed his index finger against his thumb, healing it.

Enclosing his lips around the opening of the vial, he blew with all his might and let go. Its contents flew out in a gust, filling the room with wind, mist, and glitter. Sounds of gentle, melodious chimes and sweetly singing bells filled the air. Arlend had to squint a couple times to keep from getting it into his eyes. Gradually, the sparkling fog lifted.

Suddenly, all sounds and movement ceased. Arlend opened his eyes and looked around. Each of the candles was lit with a perfectly rounded, unmoving flame.

Arlend waited a few moments. The flames stood still. Sure, it was a great show, but *why?* "People have too much time on their hands," Arlend mumbled to himself, shaking his head. He decided to go look for a means to rid himself of the useless little fires.

Just as he turned to leave, a noise that was somehow a mixture between a hurricane, wind blowing through a cave, and an avalanche was heard from directly behind him. It caused the marque to jump and swirl back around.

To his alarm, the blaze had left the candles, all gathering to completely envelop the sculpture in fire. Not just any sculpture, but his prized figurine. Enraged, Arlend dashed out to get a bucket of water right away, though he knew his efforts were in vain.

"Fire!" he shouted down the hall, but none of the hired hands had arisen yet.

Arlend couldn't believe it. So much hard work and dedication ruined. He stormed in with the bucket and stopped short. Arlend felt his heartbeat come to a halt, then start again.

The fire and candles were nowhere to be seen. Before him stood no statue paused mid-step, but a living, breathing being with human flesh. She stood with her feet together, her arms relaxed at her sides. The girl blinked, her dazzling blue eyes staring back at her creator. It was all Arlend could to do to stand and ogle at this magnificent creature who had started to look around with curiosity. He took in the beauty and brilliance of this sight, whose blood had come from Arlend's own, and who, by just the very thought of her, brought a light of joy to Arlend's heart.

She turned back to Arlend, gazing at him through her inquisitive eyes.

"Hello", he said gently.

There was a pause before she spoke, "Hi". Arlend resisted the urge to pinch himself, he could not believe his senses. Her silky voice rang even sweeter than he had imagined.

Arlend had fantasized about this moment when the two would finally meet, tossing and turning imaginary conversations in his mind. But now that his dreams had become a reality, all he could do was gape speechlessly at this… this sculpture which had just come to life as a result of his breath.

"What?" she asked.

"You," Arlend replied.

She made a face and stuck out her tongue. This guy was so cheesy.

Arlend laughed. She was so funny and cute.

Needless to say, the first day was quite awkward. Arlend did seem to enjoy every moment as he watched the little girl explore her world.

The girl, however, wandered around indifferently, trying things out and touching everything within her reach. Of course she had never been anywhere else, so Jovell's array of wealth didn't mean much to her.

And then the trumpets sounded.

Oh, no. I'm in for it now, Arlend thought. "Quick," he said. "You must come to my room. I've prepared a little space where you can stay; we must not let my father see you."

"No," the girl said, heedless of his words. "I want to see what's in that room." She pointed. Dagnabit, she was talking about the treasury, where even Arlend and his siblings, the other marques and marquesas, had to have permission to enter, and only when Jovell was watching.

"I'm sorry, you can't –"

But she had already run down the hall.

"You know, it's lock –"

To his alarm, she turned the doorknob and walked right in.

How in the world…?! But there was no time to wonder. Arlend dashed into the room just in time to see her getting….Oh no…The paramount treasure, the two-foot-tall glass sculpture of the Highlander King's Royal Palace. From an upper shelf.

"Stop!" he commanded.

"Nuh-uh. I want to play with it."

"Child, that is – "

"Don't come closer, or I may break it!"

Now, by no means did she mean that. And Arlend could clearly tell. For although he made her to have free will on purpose, he noticed at that moment something was quite strange. When he wondered what she was thinking, he just somehow *knew* exactly what was going through her mind. How that happened, he did not know, but on those grounds, he chose to step forward.

He lightly set a hand on her shoulder and tried to coax her. The rich of the Highlands often owned an Oven of Repairáge, the fifth Wonder. Arlend's family owned two. He was confident that even if it did break, he could simply put it in the oven, push a button, and voilà, good as new. The contraption could fix *anything*, as long as it fit inside and was not touched by blood. But what if Jovell heard the commotion? Things would not be well for him and his little girl, mostly her. And how he cared for that girl! The realization came to him that as he was putting all those hours of hard work to her making, he had come to love her like no other, as though she were his own child.

"No!" she stated defiantly.

"You have to, or –"

She whirled around and punched him square in the face. To do so, she had to let go with one hand, which wrecked the balance of the object in her left hand. It crashed to the floor between them as blood gushed out of Arlend's nose onto the same spot.

And then he sensed Jovell's footsteps coming down the hall.

17
Shattering

Duque Jovell appeared in the doorway of the treasury. Holding his bloody nose, Arlend tried not to meet eyes with the ruler. There wasn't much in the world Arlend was afraid of. But Jovell. Oh, and the girl…Well, he wasn't afraid of the girl, of course. He was afraid *for* her. For her life, the one he had given her.

"What on Myrada!" the ruler hollered.

And what was with his nose? Why wouldn't it heal? He needed a tissue. As in, *immediately.* But he didn't dare take even a step away from the girl. It didn't matter how she seemed to be able to hurt him like no other, even of all the people he had fought with. (What *was* with his nose?!) He needed to protect her… With what little chance he had against his father.

Arlend pulled off his shirt and held it to his nose. Jovell frowned as more blood gushed to the carpet in the process.

"Fader, I can explang," said Arlend's stuffy

voice.

"Heal your dagnabited nose first!"

"Erm…About dat…" Arlend tried again. The bleeding slowed, but didn't come to a stop. Jovell glared. Then he looked at the girl, glaring even harder. She burst into tears. Arlend's nose healed. He tossed his shirt aside (more blood to carpet) and rushed to pick her up and hold her in his arms.

She didn't know why, but the new man scared her. Really bad. And she felt bad for hitting the man who had been kind to her all along. And surprised, though grateful to him for still caring for her. In fact, he was now trying to talk to the scary guy (how brave of him!), trying to make him not angry.

As Arlend tried his best, stumbling though sentences and tripping over his own words, he noticed her wrapping her little arms around him. And how it gave him strength! Everything spoken started making more sense, at least to Arlend. But the duque just got madder and madder. When the little girl put her head on his shoulder, it was the last straw.

Arlend pulled on his shirt and darted out the

door holding the girl. Through the hallway and down the stairs he dashed. Exiting the doors, he stole a glace behind. Already, Jovell was hot at his heels. Out the gate. The stupid trumpets sounded. Then again, almost immediately following the first sound, signaling to Arlend he was fighting a losing battle.

Clutching her tightly, he sprinted at 25 mph towards the mud swamp, past the forest to the east of the city. The folks on the streets puzzled to themselves as the three went by in a blur.

"Was that Marque Arlend?"

"What was he holding?"

"Dagnabit, he's training to beat us all at the races tomorrow! "

"Double Dagnabit, he'll beat us all with flying – "

A shocked moment of silence. *Duque Jovell, too?!*

And did they think that was outlandish. But thought that lasted only until the duque came running back in the other direction.

Arlend risked another glance behind. To his surprise, the duque was nowhere in sight. But he couldn't take any chances, despite his being extremely short of breath.

"Are you doing alright?" he panted.

"I'm scared. What's going to happen?"

Arlend wished he knew. He had been running for 3 hours nonstop while toiling endlessly with trying to think of ways to plead with Jovell once caught. But he had never thought of… Had he really outrun the duque? Now, where would they go? Surely he'd get to them eventually.

Then, beyond the trees, the mud swamp came into sight.

"Child…" he said softly. "I don't know. But no matter what happens, I'll do everything I possibly can to keep you safe. I promise." She squeezed him tightly as he stepped into the swamp. As his foot sank in, so did the realization that Jovell had probably somehow… No, it couldn't be. He pushed the thought out of his mind. Sloshing through, the pace slowed immensely. He had never been in the area, but 25 years of his early life spent in learning and study had equipped him with exhaustive knowledge of the geography and languages of the entire world. He recalled that the swamp was about ten miles from west to east, and on the other side, a bay of the ocean, with the Junglicle Peninsula to the south. But so what? Then what?

"When is this going to be over?" she asked. Both the escape and the swamp, realized Arlend, inadvertently delving into her mind.

"The swamp is about ten miles, and as for – "

"How much is a mile?"

Oh. She had meant time, not distance. He gently told her, "What you mean to say is, how long will it take for us to travel a mile?"

"Yes, that." How did he know?

"Hmm…" He quickly did the math in his head. "At this pace, about half an hour." Soon, the swamp was nearly waist-deep, even for Arlend, who was on the tall side. He had to put all his concentration into walking through the swamp and avoiding the venomous creatures slithering on the murky surface, all while trying to keep his precious out of the muck. And so he didn't see what was waiting for him on the other side. "Uh…Um…" she searched.

"Arlend," he helped.

"Yeah. A-Arlend?"

"Yes?"

"Wh-what's that?"

"What's what?" he muttered, still looking down at his surroundings.

"O-over there."

He looked up. At the other side of the swamp was a helicopter bearing the royal seal. (This was after helicopters.) Without a second thought, he turned and leapt in the other direction.

"Halt!!" Duque Jovell mandated, stepping from among the throng with two of the soldiers. There would be no explaining now, no fair trial. His command in the Highlands was second only to the king – if the duque was against you, no one was for you.

That girl whimpered. *Why him again?*

Shouts of *What do I do?! What do I do?!* Pounded in Arlend's mind.

"Arlend," Jovell's voice boomed. "Come here and I won't hurt you."

Arlend had his doubts, but it seemed he had no choice. What happened to those good old days…

Arlend was about twelve at the time of the event. Childhood was beginning to come to an end, yielding to that defining time when trusted guidance was so needed.

"Touchdown!" he shouted. Jovell, the village sword maker, laughed.

"Not for long!" Jovell ran in to make the play. His little boy was growing in both stature and intelligence. At 14 mph, both he and his brother Kaedan could outrun most of the other boys their age in the village. That would be an understatement when it came to fencing, though. *Perhaps I should find them a good trainer,* he thought. *They could become fine competitors someday.* But deep down, he knew it was only a dream their family of eight simply couldn't afford.

After a good game of ball, the two sat on the front porch for some lemonade. Their lives weren't fancy, but they had everything they needed and a great family. Then, the trumpets sounded to state the presence of Important People. To the surprise of those standing by, some messengers of the king marched up to Jovell. One stepped forward, dramatically flaring out a scroll, and announced:

"Thou be blessed, O Jovell DonMateo to heareth upon thy ear of good tidings due unto thee.

His majesty King Archibald XXIVX hath Googled his family tree and hath found thee to be of royal lineage. The duque hath passeth away without heir, as thee may have heardeth and thy king hath selected thee to be his duque." (This was after Google.)

He went on and on and on about long-lost family relations, accepting royal position, et cetera, et cetera, but it all went in one ear and out the other for Arlend, who was stunned. This was every kid's dream, to be discovered to truly be so-and-so of importance.

The impulsive Jovell accepted right away. *Now I'll have the means to hire a great coach for Arlend! And buy a bow with arrows for Marta... and...and...*

But life as their family knew it was never the same again. No longer was Arlend's father a football-playing, tuck-in-at-night kind of dad. Before they knew it, he had fallen into the world of strict formality, regulations, rules, and more rules. The worst of all was the pride of ruling over everyone. Dinner conversations became political debates. Time out-talks became hard to distinguish from court trials. No more "That a boy!" with a pat on the back, but plenty of harsh punishments for every little thing gone wrong. No more laughter or games between the children and their father.

He still…seemed to care, buying them the best of everything money could give…But most of the times, it was as if he were no longer their dad. Only their duque.

Arlend now found himself out of the swamp, standing face-to-face with this duque who was once his caring dad. The one who now cared for nothing more than Arlend's championships in fencing, and elevating the family name, that was. Arlend remembered that deep down, he still loved his father. If only…

"Dad…" he started. "Please, I – "

"Arlend," he boomed sternly. "You know this… this creature will only bring trouble to you and the nation."

"The nation! Your Highness, she's a little girl! A wonderful one at that. She's harmless, she – "

"She broke the glass castle permanently and punched you!"

"Father, I – "

"She will distract you from fencing, your true passion."

"Father. I love fencing. But can fencing love me back? Can fencing – "

"Arlend. Don't argue with me. Put it down."

Arlend's sword dropped to the ground.

"Not that! *It*."

Arlend's eyes narrowed. "*She*."

"Whatever! Put that thing down!"

"No."

"Arlend!"

"No!" He was as defiant as he had never been before. Or dared to be.

Jovell tried to act as if he were calming down. "Arlend. You know I'm doing this for your good."

"Do you really know what's good for me?"

"Art is useless, my son. The only art you should concern –"

"Too late." Arlend glanced at her. "She is no longer just a painting or sculpture. You can take all those from me. But please, Your Highness, I beg of you –"

"It will only bring you harm. And distraction. Now, give it to me. I'll dispose of it humanely…"

"Never."

"What!" All anger returned to the duque's voice, even more vehemently than before. "Will you defy your duque?" He turned to the soldiers. "Take it from him."

In a fraction of a second, Arlend whirled around, set the girl down behind him and spun back to face them while picking up his sword. With that, neither of the soldiers dared to step closer.

"Go on now, how hard can it be?" urged the duque. Pretty hard, however. It wasn't everyday a guard was ordered to fight a champion. That was, until he motioned for more soldiers.

Dagnabit, Arlend thought, drawing his sword and stepping forward to put distance between the girl and the fight that was to be. The six men drew their swords. Arlend felt sick to his stomach. Jovell shook his head.

"Just get me that thing behind him!"

"Don't even try," came Arlend, waving his sword wildly in the air, hoping to intimidate. Two of the soldiers cautiously stepped toward Arlend, sword held straight out. Arlend swung, knocking both of their swords ajar with a clang. The two struggled to keep a grip on their weapons as three more jumped in to help, surrounding Arlend from all sides.

His mind shut off. Suddenly, all he knew was to fence. On automatic, his sword flew this way and that, quicker thrusts and stronger jabs shot out from Arlend like never before. A cacophony of clanging metal filled the air. Even Jovell forgot about everything, impressed with Arlend's performance.

"Yeah! That's my boy! You get them!" he called.

The soldiers now knew nothing but survival. Except for one, the guard who had stayed out of the fight. Going unnoticed and with the knowledge that Arlend would be unable to move anywhere anyway, he dodged the avid fighters and carried out the duque's original command.

Arlend snapped back just a minute too late.

"Hey! That's mine!"

All the soldiers backed off to turn in surprise to the sixth.

Arlend froze to look at the girl, who was petrified with fear. You would be, too, if you were a five-year-old girl standing about thirty feet away from your only source of love and alone with the duque who was after your life. Not desiring to arouse the soldiers, Arlend started to inch towards the girl, bit by bit. But what was the ruler holding in his hand?

It was a tiny, glowing orb of light which was slowly growing in mass. The sixth Wonder, a horrible Wonder: the Shockwave. Only two had been found and turned in to the government in Jovell's whole lifetime, a good thing for something with such potency. Receiving a Shockwave meant certain death, and an excruciatingly painful one at that.

Arlend dove towards the girl.

"Run, run!" he shouted to her.

No use. Jovell held the ball, now the size of a football above his head. And squeezed. It stretched out into a thin line, cutting through the air towards the girl.

Arlend was ten feet away from her.

And the shockwave, two feet.

With an impenetrable forest to her left and the ocean to her right, the girl ran ahead for dear life.

The shockwave reached a single foot behind her.

Arlend ducked, pulling the girl to the ground with him. But the Shockwave curved to follow her. On the ground, the marque scrambled to cover her body with his.

And then, bam. Explosion of light and energy. Impact. Arlend grimaced as it penetrated his skin. And then, an ear-splitting shriek pierced the air. Her shriek. And then it stopped. Silence.

Shaking, Arlend barely had the strength to keep himself from collapsing on top of the girl. He forced himself off her with great difficulty and fell beside her, looking on. Her eyes were closed, with no sign of life about her still form. *How could this be?* He asked himself. *I did everything possible to receive the worst part of the shock.*

Arlend never cried. On the day he was born, Arlend screamed through the sobs of the others. When he was stabbed in the chest during a fight, he pulled the sword out and healed. He hid his pain and kept right on fighting. But this was more than he could bear.

The tears rolled across his face at his first and greatest loss, he reached out with his last ounce of strength. Grasping her little left hand in his, he gave her a name which meant "the light of my heart" in the ancient language of the Highlands lost to most.

"The light of your heart…" Faylin sniffled, the tears flowing rapidly down. "Heartlight. Me?"

Arlend nodded. "Yes, Faylin, my heartlight. Fay, while I've been waiting here, I contacted George C. Quincy… He gave me instructions, and…I've equipped you with all you'll need so you can survive without me. Fay, I love you." His voice strained, and his eyes closed. His skin became paler and paler as he told her about her creation, and now it appeared deathly white.

"Nooooo! Arly!" Faylin sobbed.

"Now, now, calm down, or you'll ruin all that he has done to let you live." The duque tried to sound firm despite his own eyes starting to well up.

"Noooo! I don't want to live! Not without Arlend!" she cried. "I love you, Arlend!" she wailed.

Jovell left to get nurses.

Some nights in her slavery, she had cried until she thought she could not cry any longer. When Gunther took her, she felt she could not cry any harder. But now, she knew the meaning of the phrase, 'the tears will never stop'. She couldn't live on. This time, she knew she wouldn't.

For the first time in her life, Arlend was wrong. He hadn't provided her with everything she needed. She didn't just need blood, or something from his oxygen she lacked. She needed *him*. She needed him there to dry her tears, to kiss her goodnight and to protect her. She needed him to laugh with and to hold on to and to carry her through life's troubles. To tell her she was special, and loved, beyond anything else in the universe. Even life.

She tore away the tubes and wires, leaping into his arms. She willed with all her might that those arms would hold her close once more, and that he would awaken and whisper in her eat that it was all going to be okay.

But he didn't.

Never in her life had she felt so miserable. She would rather *anything* else happen to her, anything but this.

She thought back to the time Vizain nearly beat her to death. Even that was better. Why? Because Arlend came. He picked her up and healed her, and….

Suddenly, Faylin thought of something. Other Highlanders could only heal themselves. But Arlend had healed her. If she was truly the work of a Highlander's hands, in the place of a Highlander, then she too was a Highlander. Maybe she could heal Arlend.

She thought about what Arlend had done. '… Just held you and wished so hard that you'd get better…' he had once told her. But it hadn't worked when Faylin didn't have much blood left. Then, it came to her. *That* was why he could heal her: when he made her, it was his blood he'd used. They were not only joined in heart, but they had one blood. Faylin figured that since she was smaller, then Arlend probably still had *some* blood left. She had to give it a try.

She wrapped her arms tightly around him and squeezed her eyes shut. "Let my love heal you," she prayed.

And then, she wished, she yearned, she willed. He just *had* to get better. She wanted it so much. She wanted to be with him more than anything. More than life.

Like wishing hard in those twilight moments, just before drifting to sleep, his arms and voice surrounded her. Was she dreaming? Were they dead? Faylin dared to open her eyes.

About the Author

Annie Renfay is a talented and creative writer who's always got her head in the clouds and her nose in a book. She first started writing at the age of 12 and was greatly inspired by her 9th grade creative writing teacher, Mrs. Blair, and the community formed in her class. She has been published previously as a poet in a magazine and several anthologies, and has held a position in the children's department of her local library. She is also the editor of the book *Cat Spell* by Zackary Oliver, the same genius whose creative suggestions helped her immensely throughout the writing of this book. Her Web site is www.annierenfay.com.

Printed in the United States
137419LV00001B/1/P